The Cats That Told a Fortune

Karen Anne Golden

Copyright

This book or eBook is a work of fiction. Names, characters, places and incidents are products of the author's imagination or are used fictitiously. Any resemblance to actual events, locales, persons or cats, living or dead, is entirely coincidental.

Edited by Vicki Braun.

Cover design by Christy Carlyle of Gilded Heart Design.

Copyright © 2014 Karen Anne Golden

ISBN-13: 978-1500268305

ISBN-10: 1500268305

Dedication

To my mom, Mildred Maffett Golden

&

My grandmothers:

Eulah Orvenia Sowers Maffett

&

Pearl Elizabeth Golden

Acknowledgements

My appreciation goes out to my sister, Linda Golden, who has been a tremendous help throughout this process.

Thanks to Vicki Braun, my editor, who meticulously edited this book. Vicki also edited the first two books of *The Cats that . . .* Cozy Mystery series. Also, special thanks to Christy Carlyle, my book cover designer. Christy is a genius at taking a photograph and incorporating it into a fun cover.

Thank you Pauline Nicolaï, my beta reader from the Netherlands. If it weren't for the Internet, I would never have met you. Thank you, Melissa McGee, for coordinating the other beta team readers: Catherine Scott, Tammy Richardson, Mona Kekstadt, Mary Hesselgesser-Wright and Debbie Perry. Melissa also read the book and made valid suggestions regarding paranormal investigations.

I want to express my appreciation to my family and friends. Thanks to my brother, Bob Golden, who showed me how to use a Glock.

Thanks to my friend Sandy and her late husband, Carl DeVault, who took me to my very first Covered Bridge Festival. Also to my late father, who introduced my husband and me to our first Hoosier fish fry.

I am grateful to my rescued cats, without whose antics I wouldn't have a story. Special mention of Redmond, who can open many kinds of locks, and Rusty, who graces my Facebook pages with lots of pix of Rusty being Rusty.

Table of Contents

Prologue

It was a crisp fall evening in the small town of Erie, Indiana. The full moon bathed the eastern side of the pink mansion – a Queen Anne Victorian built in 1897 – in a cool, bluish light. On Lincoln Street, the remaining maple trees that survived the tornado clung to the last of their brilliantly colored leaves. The sidewalks and street were littered with them, and the front drainage ditch was full. The surrounding neighbors' front porches were seasonally decorated with bales of hay, scarecrows and Halloween carved pumpkins. Katherine Kendall, the young heiress to the Colfax fortune, joined the fun and moved her late great aunt Orvenia's cast-stone gargoyles from the attic to either side of the front porch landing. She'd tied orange and black bows around the ornate, winged beasts, which now graced the mansion with a Halloween spirit.

During the day, tourists walked up and down the street, snapping pictures of the historical homes and autumn leaves, but mostly of the pink painted lady that had become known as the "pink murder house." Because of the Colfax mansion's history, and the crimes committed in the house, Erie was attracting more sightseers than usual – mostly out-of-towners heading south on U.S. 41 to attend the Covered Bridge Festival in Brook County.

After the tornado severely damaged the mansion, Katherine rented a restored bungalow. She and her cats clung to living there as long as they could, but were forced by the terms of her great aunt's will – a relative she had never met – to return to the pink mansion in late July. It had been repaired and restored to its former glory. The reconstruction of the porte cochere or carport was nearly complete. Margie, the wife of the estate's handyman, Cokey Cokenberger, was finishing the detailed painting of the balusters to match the four-color paint scheme.

But life inside went on as usual. Katherine and her cats had finally settled in. Abra, the tall, svelte seal-point littermate of Scout, had been performing with a famous magician in the Catskills when she was stolen years earlier and later abandoned at an animal shelter. Now she was miraculously reunited with her sister. Abra was adjusting well to the other felines, but still had an occasional spat with Abby, the Abyssinian, who hadn't quite gotten used to the hyperactive newcomer. Scout and Abra were joined at the hip like Siamese twins and didn't leave each other's side. Katherine tried to change Abra's name, but the stubborn former Hocus Pocus performer didn't want any part of it. So, Katz nicknamed her Shadow, but mostly called her Abra. Lilac was happy as long as her bear was within reach. The lilac-point Siamese was Abby's best friend. Visitors could usually find Lilac and Abby basking together in a sunny spot on one of the mansion's many windowsills, or up high on one of the carved-wood window valances. However, Iris, affectionately known as Miss Siam – a dark blue-eyed seal-point from a swanky cattery in Manhattan – was a different story. When Abra arrived, she became depressed. Katherine took her to the vet, Dr. Sonny. He suspected Iris resented Abra because of her connection to Scout, who rarely made time for her old buddy. As a result, Miss Siam became clingy to her human, and followed her everywhere.

After great uncle William's bones were interred in the Colfax mausoleum, the mansion seemed to be at peace with itself. There were no ghostly intrusions in the middle of the night. No wafts of cold, icy air when certain rooms were entered. The cats were no longer startled by unseen forces.

But Katherine was still troubled by a sense of foreboding that something bad was going to happen. In four months, she would inherit millions from the Colfax estate. She was well on her way to meeting the requirement of caring for her great aunt's cat,

Abby. She should be on top of the world. Close

friends were okay. The cats were fine. She was

dating a wonderful man. Yet she was overcome

with apprehension.

*   *   *

Earlier that evening, somewhere south of the

pink mansion, Brook County sheriff's deputies

found the lifeless body of a young woman. She was

the first victim of a serial killer. More would follow

in what became known as the Festival Murders.

Chapter One

On this cold fall evening, in the pink mansion's living room, Katherine and Jake sat in matching wingback chairs. It was their weekend movie night. Katherine had picked the last movie, so it was Jake's turn. He chose a recent release zombie movie. Katherine wasn't too keen on watching it, but cradling Iris in her arms made it easier. Jake sat holding two cats, one in the crook of each arm. Every time the volume got louder and the action grew more violent, Abby and Lilac would bury their heads in his arms. Scout and Abra were elsewhere in the mansion, doing their routine reconnaissance to explore every nook and cranny of the old house. They had already made one sweep, but began all over again, trotting shoulder-to-shoulder and looking like mirror images. A nearby kitchen timer went off, which announced intermission and snack time.

When Jake started to get up, Lilac and Abby jumped to the floor. They both stretched, then launched from the floor to the fireplace mantel to the window valance, where they watched their persons below.

"Do you want pizza or chips?" Jake asked. "I brought one of those mini-pizzas I can nuke."

"Chips would be nice. I'd help you," Katherine said, then added innocently, "but I'm very busy right now with Iris."

"Oh, I can see that," Jake said with an amused glint in his eye. He walked to the kitchen and returned with potato chips, French onion dip, nachos and melted cheese. "Here's a pop," he said, handing her a Diet Coke. When he put the nachos on the side table, Iris bolted off Katherine's lap, snatched a chip, and ran out of the room.

"Hey, you rascal, come back here," Jake called to the feline thief.

Katherine giggled. "She doesn't eat it. She just licks the salt off. I'll get it tomorrow with the Hoover," she said, then asked, "Before we go back to the movie, can we talk about the Halloween party?"

"Oh, good idea," Jake said, sitting down. "What day is it?"

"October 25th – it's a Saturday."

"Well, that's good, because I may have to proctor an exam on the 24th."

Katherine smiled, happy that Jake was back doing what he loved – after taking a sabbatical from the university to deal with his late wife's fatal cancer – and was now getting back on track with his life.

"I hope Colleen and Mario are coming, so I can finally meet them," Jake said.

Katherine took a sip of her drink. "Colleen is coming, but not Mario. They broke up. She's bringing her brother, Jacky."

"When did that happen?" Jake asked curiously.

"Just a few days ago. I didn't mention it because I thought they were just having a lovers' quarrel."

"Sounds like drama. What happened?"

"Without warning, Mario announced he was moving back to Italy. He asked Colleen to go with him, but when he didn't propose, she said 'no.' Without a wedding ring on her finger, Colleen told him she didn't want to leave the States. She's devastated."

"The fool should have asked her to marry him," Jake commented. "Who else is on the invitation list?"

"Cokey and Margie. Professor Watson."

"Oh, Wayne asked if he could bring his new girlfriend."

"Is she into metal detecting, too?" Katherine asked, remembering the tall professor who was a dead ringer for Buddy Holly, and how he found a million dollars in gold coins.

"I haven't met her, but he talks about her all the time. Her name is Leslie. I'll get her address for the invitation."

"Perfect! I also have Michelle Pike, from the library, on the list. Since Beatrice is behind bars, we've become good friends."

"It's just my opinion, but should it be boy-girl, boy-girl? How old is Colleen's brother?" Jake asked.

"Boy-girl? I've never heard of that before," Katherine said, slightly amused. "Jacky's in his early thirties."

"Well, that leaves Michelle out, because she's too young."

"What are we running here – a dating service? Michelle is older than she looks. She's twenty-four. Sometimes women like older men," Katherine said, tongue-in-cheek.

"Oh, that's a good one," Jake teased. He pointed at William Colfax's portrait hanging next to the fireplace. "Wasn't he eighty-something when he married your great aunt Orvenia? And wasn't she seventeen?"

Katherine smirked, "Yes, Professor."

"It's not like we're pairing them off, but my cousin from Shaleville would love to come. You'll meet him next week when we go to the Covered Bridge Festival in Brook County."

"What's his name?"

"Daryl. One of the many Cokenbergers in this neck of the woods."

"Does he look like you?" Katherine inquired with a sly smile.

Jake reached over and pinched her arm. "Daryl's twenty-five. He's got blond hair and blue eyes."

"He sounds handsome."

"The women love him," Jake said enticingly.

"Oh, really?" she asked, "and why is that?"

"Because he's a Cokenberger," Jake announced, having fun.

"Too funny. I know Colleen is beside herself in boyfriend drama, but keeping with your boy-girl equation, maybe they'll hit it off, or just be friends."

"Matchmaker," he teased. "Speaking of friends, are you inviting Mark?" Jake asked.

"I'm not sure yet. Last time I talked to him, he said he was super busy with his law practice. I haven't seen him since the last distribution from the estate," she said, then hesitated. "He'll probably want to see Colleen while she's in town."

"How long is she going to stay?"

"This I don't know. I hope a couple of weeks."

A loud crash came from the adjoining room.

Katherine flung herself out of the chair and hurried to investigate. Jake followed her. Scout or Abra – probably both – had knocked off a box of Halloween party decorations that was on the marble-top curio cabinet. Abra had tugged out a cat-size purple cape and was racing around the room with it clutched in her V-shaped jaw. Scout chased after her, but wasn't fast enough to catch the fleeing feline.

Jake was too busy laughing to catch Abra, who flew up the stairs lickety-split.

Katherine said, "This would be a great picture for the cover of the invitation!" She grabbed her smartphone and began snapping photos.

Jake said, "I'll grab her and put the cape on her."

"Good luck," Katherine said, under her breath.

The incredibly fast Siamese ran from room-to-room with Jake at her heels. Finally he caught her and held her for a minute, talking to her in a soft voice. "Raw," Abra replied sweetly.

Abra was used to being dressed up in costume, so she didn't resist when Jake put the cape on her. Instead of fleeing the scene like the other cats would have, she stood tall, with her triangular, wedge-shaped face pointing up in a regal manner.

Katherine hurriedly snapped several more photos.

Scout became jealous of Abra getting attention, so she muttered something in 'Siamese' and snatched the cape off Abra.

Katherine took a picture of that as well, and then picked up Scout and gave her a kiss on the back of her neck. "Magic cat," she said affectionately.

Scout wriggled out of her arms and hopped back into the Halloween party box.

"Scout, I really need to put the box away," Katherine mildly scolded.

"Waugh," Scout complained. Pawing through the box, the inquisitive Siamese found a deck of Tarot cards. She clenched the deck in her teeth and leapt out. As Scout shook the box, the cards spilled out. With lightning speed, Abra started scattering them on the floor. The glossy cards slid easily on the carpet, so Scout and Abra launched into a game of card hockey. Lilac and Abby heard the commotion, launched from their valance perch, and joined in the fun.

Jake stifled a laugh, "I guess this means you need to hire a fortune teller."

"Where am I going to find a fortune teller in Erie?" Katherine wrinkled her nose and smiled.

Jake shrugged. "Angie's list? Google search?"

Scout dropped a fang-punctured card on Katherine's shoe.

Reaching down, Katherine picked it up and observed, "It's the Wheel of Fortune card."

"Does that mean you're going to be on TV?" Jake asked facetiously.

"It looks like it has a sphinx on it," she said to Jake, and then to Scout, "Is that why you picked it, sweetie, because of the sphinx?"

"Ma-waugh," Scout said indifferently.

16

"I'll have to go online and look up what it means," Katherine said. "Okay, let's get back to the movie."

When Jake and Katherine walked into the living room, they gasped. Iris had dumped the bowl of nacho chips and spread them throughout the large room.

Iris sat innocently on Katherine's chair.

Jake joked, "I guess she had her own game of hockey."

Katherine said, "I'll get the Hoover!"

"I'll get more chips," Jake answered.

Chapter Two

It was the first day of computer training at the pink mansion. Although Katherine had proposed the classroom design the previous spring, the project had run into various snags. Windows were ordered, didn't fit, and had to be shipped back. The electrical work was not up to code and had to be rewired. The new HVAC was difficult to install. But now in October, the new classroom was finally ready for the first group of students.

Katherine had poured over numerous applications. It was difficult to select four candidates for the first course, so she wrote their names on tiny folded cards and dropped them in a large crystal bowl. Scout and Abra were eager to help with the selection. They fished out a card, played with it for a while and then pierced it with a fang mark – sometimes with multiple punctures. Scout preferred to clutch the card in her brown paws and chew on it, while Abra daintily bit the corner. Katherine selected five fang-marked cards, the fifth being a backup in case one of the other students failed to complete the course.

Katherine had decided to first teach the basics of computing. The class would meet twice a week, with the second session devoted to practice. The course would last four weeks. Students would be introduced to various hardware, standalones, laptops, notebooks, and tablets, then move on to keyboarding, word processing, and creating spreadsheets. Each workstation was equipped with a large-screen monitor and a pull-out shelf for a keyboard and wireless mouse. A printer was connected to each station, and a desktop computer was tucked below, on a shelf. Katherine was a pro at designing efficient, comfortable workspaces, because one of her tasks in Manhattan had been to make each work cubicle an efficient place to work –

from the height of the keyboard, to the ergonomic design of the office chair.

Katherine was excited about the first day, but also a little bit nervous. Her last training session at her old job in New York had been eight months ago. After she unlocked the classroom door, she made sure each desktop copy stand held the day's lesson. Realizing she'd forgotten to add paper to the tray on her printer, she left the room to walk into the far part of the basement where she kept office supplies. She was busy removing a ream of paper from the case when someone quietly walked up behind her. With the ream in hand, she turned and screamed, dropping the paper on the floor.

"What do you want?" she asked, frightened.

"I'm sorry. I didn't mean to scare you. I'm your new student, Glen. I was looking for the restroom," he apologized.

Katherine felt her heart pounding and said firmly, "It's located right outside the classroom." She didn't move until the student left.

Creepy, she thought. *How strange I didn't hear him. He was practically right on top of me.*

Returning to the classroom, she found two students sitting at their workstations, making small talk. Glen strolled in and took a seat. Katherine was loading the paper in her printer when a voluptuous woman in her early thirties stormed in loudly. She wore a low-neck sweater, with cleavage that would rival any geologic fissure. Dressed entirely in pink, she sported enough "bling" to cause temporary blindness. She threw a haughty glance around the room, spotted Katherine behind her desk, and laughed, "Oh, ha! Ha! Sorry, I'm late, Teach." She threw her large Coach handbag on the floor and noisily sat down. "I take it this is where I'm supposed to sit," she smirked.

"Yes," Katherine said. "My name is Katherine Kendall. You can call me Katz."

"Oh, ha! Ha! What a stupid name," the student stated, then said sheepishly, "I was just kidding."

Katherine glared at her and continued, "I'd like to get to know all of you, so let's spend a few minutes introducing ourselves."

The overbearing woman said, "My name is Barbie. People call me Barbie! Get it?"

"What do you wish to take from this course?" Katherine asked, as she imagined giving Barbie a smack.

"Oh, a tour of the pink murder house," Barbie blurted, then instantly countered, "Just kidding."

With difficulty, Katherine ignored the remark and moved on. "There were numerous applications for this course. We held a lottery and selected the fab four." *Lottery*, Katherine thought, *with feline assistants.* "Let me ask you again, what do you want to learn?"

"Duh, about computers," Barbie said, rolling her eyes.

Katherine ignored this remark as well and looked at Glen, who moments earlier had scared her half to death. He was in his early twenties and had piercing blue eyes. He sported a shaved head. His hair had to be light, because he had very bushy blond eyebrows. Dressed entirely in black, he had a gleaming gold earring in his ear. He was sitting next to Barbie. Katherine asked, "Glen, why are you taking this course?"

"Oh," he answered quickly. "I applied so I can try for the manager's job at the restaurant."

"What, flipping hamburgers ain't good enough for you?" Barbie observed under her breath.

The young man threw a dirty look aimed at Barbie and said, "I'd watch it if I were you."

Katherine realized her first day of class was not going very well. "Glen, for the class, what's your last name?"

"Frye."

Barbie said sarcastically, "Fry burger, get it?"

"Enough, Barbie," Katherine snapped. "Can we dispense with the comments? You're holding up the class."

"Yes, Barbie," Michelle from the library said. Michelle was wearing her signature black turtleneck, black tights, and black ballerina slippers.

"Oh, touchy-touchy," Barbie commented.

"Michelle, what do you wish to gain from the course?" Katherine asked.

"I think it would help me to do a better job at the library."

Barbie brought her hand up to her mouth like she was going to say something, but didn't.

24

"Good reason," Katherine said. She directed her attention to a waif of a girl sitting next to Michelle. "I'm Leslie," the girl spoke in a tiny voice. Her hair was bright red and cut very short in layers. She wore large, rhinestone eyeglasses. "I'd like to learn more about computers so I can get a part-time admin job at the university."

"Okay," Katherine said. "These are great reasons. My goal is to get you where you want to be." She then began teaching about the hardware. "This tower contains the brain of the computer. The computer brain is a microprocessor called the Central Processing Unit, or CPU. It contains millions of transistors that manipulate data." Katherine continued her explanation, until two tall, svelte Siamese trotted in. Together in one fluid bound, Scout and Abra jumped on Katherine's desk. "Waugh," Scout said to Abra's "raw."

"Ahhh," Leslie said, "Wayne told me you had cats. They're beautiful. What kind are they?"

"Siamese," Katherine said proudly. She was going to say more, but Barbie cut her off.

"Siamese are mean like those cats in *Lady and the Tramp*." Barbie then launched into a terrible rendition of the "We are Siamese" song.

Glen leaned over and muttered, "Only mean to people like you, Barbie."

Scout and Abra stared at the rude student. Scout's whip-like tail was thumping angrily on the desk.

Katherine said, "If it's all right, we'll let them stay until they get bored. Then they'll take their leave."

"Okay by us," Michelle said. "They're really cute."

Barbie asked, "Did they cost a lot? How much money would you make if you sold them?"

Katherine looked aghast and said hastily, "My cats are my family. They're in their forever home. I would *never* sell them."

"Oh, ha! Ha!" Barbie said loudly. "I was just kidding."

Once the hardware part of the lecture was finished, Katherine moved onto the basics of keyboarding. "In this class, you'll break the habit of hunting and pecking. I will show you the correct position of your fingers on the keyboard. Take a look at your copy stand. The first diagram illustrates the middle horizontal row of the keyboard that begins with the letter A. This is known as the home row."

"This is stupid," Barbie broadcasted. "I don't need to learn this. I'm fine with my thumbs. Look," she said, pounding the keyboard with her thumbs.

"I bet you're good with your thumbs," Glen said suggestively. "But will you please shut up," he implored.

"You don't tell me to shut up, burger slinger," Barbie said, standing up.

Katherine had grown furious. Grabbing a twenty dollar bill out of her desk drawer, which was the low cost of the course, she briskly walked over to Barbie. "Do you know what a New York minute is?"

"Why should I? I live in Indiana," Barbie said cynically.

Katherine quickly evaluated the size of this rude woman, who clearly outweighed her by two to one. She wondered which way she should duck if Barbie threw a punch.

"A New York minute is the amount of time it's going to take you to gather your stuff and get out of my class," Katherine snapped.

"But I paid. You can't do that!" Barbie said indignantly.

Katherine slammed the twenty on the workstation. "Yes, I can. Now leave," she demanded.

"Fine," Barbie said, yanking her handbag off the floor and heading to the door. "This is a stupid waste of time anyway. And by the way, your short hair looks like crap! Jennifer Lawrence you ain't." Barbie slammed the door after her.

"Thank you, Lord," Glen said, raising his hands in the air.

"I second that," Michelle said irritably.

"Yay," Leslie added. "People can be so rude."

Katherine regained her composure and apologized, "Let's move on. How many of you already know the basics of keyboarding?"

The three remaining students raised their hands.

"Okay, let's try an exercise. I want to find out how many words per minute you type. On your copy stand are several paragraphs of text. I want you to type it. I'll time you. I'll give you a few seconds to get ready. Once you begin typing I'll call time in one minute."

The students put their fingers on their keyboards.

"Ready, get set. Go," Katherine said, clicking her stopwatch.

*   *   *

The two hours wore on until it was time to end the class. The students seemed to appreciate what they had learned, and left with a sense of accomplishment.

As Leslie headed to the door, she said, "Wayne and I can't wait for the party. It sounds like so much fun."

"You're welcome," Katherine said, smiling.

Michelle lingered behind and gave Katherine a serious look, "Hey, watch out for that Barbie woman. Do you know who she is?"

"No, just a loud mouth, ne'er-do-well."

"She's the daughter of Sam Sanders. He's got tons of kids, from several different marriages, mostly sons. Barbie is his only daughter, and she's spoiled rotten."

"Got that last part. Who's Sam Sanders?" Katherine asked.

"He's the patriarch of one of the biggest crime families in Erie."

"What?" Katherine asked, disbelieving what she had heard.

"Yep, from meth to massage parlors," Michelle said, continuing, "I guess since you're from New York, you know about the mob. Well, Sam Sanders is Erie's version of John Gotti. So watch your back."

"Good to know," Katherine said. "Thanks for the heads up. What did Glen's remark to Barbie about 'thumbs' mean? The way he said it sounded like an innuendo."

Michelle giggled, "Barbie runs one of the massage parlors. Actually, it's a brothel!"

Katherine looked shocked. "Oh, my God!" she said. "Where is it?"

"Oh, a few miles north of here, off the main drag. Barbie's got a trailer in a run-down trailer court."

"Run-down? But she was carrying an expensive Coach bag," Katherine observed.

"Must do well with what she does," Michelle said with a twinkle in her eye. "Every once in a while the place gets busted. Barbie gets arrested for this, that and the other, but she 'lawyers up' and gets out of it on some technicality."

Changing the subject, Katherine said, "Speaking of 'lawyering up,' Mark Dunn told me Beatrice was sentenced last week, but he didn't elaborate." Katherine remembered the day at the Ethel cemetery when the former Erie librarian shot Wayne, Jake's metal-detecting friend.

"She did a plea bargain and got three years with probation. The prosecutor dropped the hit-and-run charge. It seems that Beatrice wasn't in the car when Carol Lombard was driven off the road. Her husband's trial is coming up soon. His attorney asked the judge for a change of venue, so the case is being tried in a different county."

"I know I haven't been over to the library lately, but did you get promoted to Beatrice's old job?"

Michelle shook her head sadly. "Nope. The board hired a gal with a degree in Library Science, so that leaves me out."

"Have you ever thought about going to the university?" Katherine asked.

"Can't afford it. I'm taking this class so I can get a better-paying job in the city. The plan is to work full-time and go to school part-time. That's my goal and I aim to achieve it!" Michelle said determinedly.

Maybe I should set up a scholarship foundation when I inherit the estate, Katherine thought. *Michelle would be my first candidate.*

Michelle gathered up her bag and started to leave. She stopped by the door and said, "Oh, I got your invitation. It was so cute with your cat wearing the purple cape. My cat wouldn't tolerate clothes," she laughed.

Katherine beamed, "That was my new Siamese, Abra. She was one of the two that blessed us with a visit earlier. She had the cape on for a split second, because her sister Scout hated it and snatched it off her."

Michelle became serious. "What do you think of Glen?"

"Why do you ask?" Katherine wondered, getting the part that Michelle was attracted to him.

"I asked him to be my guest at the party. And he said yes," Michelle said happily. She began singing Daft Punk's song "Get Lucky."

Katherine said with a wink, "Let's not get too lucky, because it's the first date."

Still singing, Michelle left, then called through the door, "See you Wednesday for the practice session."

Katherine sat back in her chair and reflected that her first class was the worst class she'd ever taught. She was curious about the Sanders family and wanted to ask Jake about them later, at lunch. She worried about possible repercussions of throwing Barbie out of her class. She desperately wanted to text her friend in New York, but figured Colleen would be too bummed out about Mario to text back.

As Katherine mounted the stairs to her office, Iris was on the other side of the partially opened door, yowling sweetly. Katherine grabbed her around the middle and gave her a kiss on top of her head. "Where are my other kids?" she called, walking to the atrium, but no other cats were present. "Must be sleeping, right, Miss Siam?" Katherine's house phone rang and she put Iris down to answer it. It was Jake.

"Hey, are you still coming to my class?" he asked.

"Of course, I wouldn't miss it."

"Great! We're still going to lunch afterwards, right?"

"Definitely. I'll see you later." Katherine hung up and immediately went upstairs to freshen up. Today was the part of Jake's course on Prohibition where he dressed up like John Dillinger, the notorious Indiana gangster. She chuckled to herself, *Geez, I hope he doesn't wear that get-up to lunch!*

*   *   *

Katherine made the trip to the city in record time. She had a lead foot when it came to the accelerator. She finally set the cruise control on the new Subaru, lest she find herself doing eighty in a fifty-five MPH zone. Arriving on campus, she couldn't find a parking space. She'd never seen so many cars, so much traffic, and so many students walking about, heading for their classes. It seemed the parking spaces required a special permit, and

since she didn't have one, she didn't relish parking
and then having her new car towed. She tried
several parking garages, but each one was full.
Pulling up along a curbed sidewalk, she lowered her
window and asked a university cop what to do. He
directed her to the outskirts of the campus to park at
the stadium parking lot. It took a full twenty
minutes to walk to the lecture hall where Jake was
teaching. She followed Jake's scribbled directions,
but got lost several times, and lamented that all the
brick buildings looked the same.

It was a typical, breezy fall day, so Katherine's
short-cropped hair was standing up on end. A quick
run into the ladies room solved that problem, but by
the time she got to the lecture hall, only a few seats
were available at the very top, in the nosebleed
section. When she walked in, Jake stood in front of
the podium, dressed like Johnny Depp in *Public
Enemies*. His haircut even matched Dillinger's.
Katherine gulped, and managed a smile. Jake smiled

back and winked. She could feel his eyes watching her as she ascended the steps. She prayed she wouldn't trip and go flying into a row, but managed to find one of the last seats available.

The class was packed. The students were lively. Katherine could tell everyone thoroughly enjoyed this part of the lecture. A gaggle of admiring female students sat in several front rows, reminding Katherine of a scene from *Raiders of the Lost Ark* in which Harrison Ford's character was teaching a class. But none of the girls had flirty messages written on their eyelids.

When the lecture was finished, Katherine patiently waited for the students to leave, then walked down the steps.

"What did you think?" Jake beamed happily.

Katherine had to refrain from running over and giving him a passionate kiss.

"I loved it! Can I take your picture?" she asked, taking her smartphone out of her pocket.

"Of course," he said, flashing his handsome Cokenberger smile.

"I want to text it to Colleen. I'll do that at lunch."

"Are you ready?" he asked, collecting his lecture notes. "I've got this great Chinese restaurant in mind. They have an incredible buffet."

"I'm starving. Is it far from here?" she asked, still exhausted from the sprint from the stadium parking lot.

"Oh, I'm parked outside the building," he answered. "By the way, you parked in the parking garage, right?"

"No, I couldn't find a spot."

"So where did you park?" Jake asked, taking her arm and leading her to the door.

"It's called the stadium."

Jake laughed. "The lower forty? Okay, we'll take the Jeep to the restaurant. Great food, but it isn't on campus. I'll drive you to your Sue-bee afterwards."

They exited the building and Jake directed Katherine to the blue Jeep Wrangler.

"I've got a faculty sticker," he chuckled. "Jump in," he said, opening the door.

Katherine climbed in and fastened her seat belt. Jake got in behind the steering wheel. He started to put the Jeep in gear, but paused and said, "Hey, I forgot to tell you something."

"What's that?"

"You were the most beautiful woman in the entire class," he said, reaching over and kissing her on the cheek.

"Ahhh," Katherine gushed.

He put the Jeep in gear and eased out into traffic. "How did your first class go?"

"It was a disaster!" Katherine answered disappointedly.

"What in the world happened?" he asked, gaining speed and putting the Jeep into second gear.

"I had an incident with one of my students, and I had to evict her from the class."

"You what?" he asked incredulously. "It's a community service for crying out loud. Who was it?"

"Barbie —"

"Oh, no," he interrupted. "Not Barbie Sanders? She's in your class?"

"Was," Katherine said. "How do you know her?" she asked with a curious side-glance.

"Well, definitely not in the way you're suggesting," he laughed. "Okay, you don't have to tell me now, but over lunch I want to hear all about it," he said soothingly. "But first, you never did tell me how you selected five students from all those applications."

When Katherine told him about Scout and Abra assisting, he couldn't stop laughing. Finally, he said, "Next time you need a better plan. Who else is in the class?"

"Michelle who works in the library, a guy named Glen Frye, and Wayne's girlfriend, Leslie."

"How strange the Siamese picked two people you either know or just met. Glen Frye is a bit of a Casanova. He's the day chef at the Erie Hotel. I played high school basketball with his older brother. But Barbie Sanders – the massage queen? Oh, no you didn't."

"Luck of the draw. Jake, I'm nervous about something."

"What could that be?" Jake said, pulling into the Chinese restaurant's crowded parking lot.

"Do you think there'll be any nasty consequences? Michelle said Barbie's dad was a crim."

"I hope not, sweet pea," he said affectionately. "The Sanders and the Cokenbergers, as the locals say, ain't friends. But, I wouldn't worry about it."

"I notified the fifth candidate – the alternate. I'm teaching the course to her later this afternoon, so she'll be able to join the rest of the class on Wednesday for the practice session."

Jake eased into a parking spot close to the restaurant's entrance.

Katherine remarked, "Incredible! What's with you and finding the closest parking spaces?"

"Well, I thought you'd want to be closer to great food than if we'd parked at the stadium and taken the bus." He chuckled again.

Katherine poked him in the ribs and thought about how fun he was. And for the first time since leaving campus, she noticed Jake was still in his Dillinger "costume." She wondered what the other patrons would think, especially if he brought along the fake tommy gun. As it turned out, no one noticed. He left his prop in the Jeep, along with the famous Dillinger straw hat.

The food was delicious. She ate too much. Jake complained that he did, too. They skipped dessert, but opened their fortune cookies and read the messages.

Jake said, "I think I got yours. It says 'A big fortune will descend upon you this year.'"

Katherine laughed, "Ha! They're wrong. Next year!" She broke her cookie open and read hers

45

aloud, "The Wheel of Good Fortune is finally turning in your direction."

"Wow, what are the odds of that?" Jake observed. "First, Scout picks out the Wheel of Fortune Tarot card; now this," Jake said, then hummed the opening bars of the *Twilight Zone* theme.

"I did a Google search on the meaning of that Tarot card. I got a headache from the fine print on interpretation. I'm supposed to have either fate smile down upon me, or there's an unwelcome change ahead. That doesn't make any sense to me. Thank you very much, Scout, for fang marking it for me," Katherine grinned.

Jake paid the bill, left a tip, and said he had a three o'clock, so he drove Katherine back to the stadium and parked next to her Subaru. He hopped out, rushed over and opened the door for her. Katherine unfastened her seat belt and slid out.

Jake said, "Thank you for showing up today. It meant a lot to me." Before she had time to answer, he kissed her lightly on the lips.

Once Katherine was seated in her vehicle, he quipped, "By the way, I like your 'New York minute' line. Next time I have to throw out a student, I'll be sure to use it."

Katherine flashed him a smile, then started her car.

Jake hopped back in his Jeep and took off.

He's amazing, Katherine thought. Before she left the stadium, she sent a text to Colleen, attaching Jake's picture. Colleen immediately texted back, "Uncanny resemblance."

Katherine had a few errands to do, but she made it back to Erie by four o'clock. The fifth student, who would replace Barbie, was coming over at five. After Katherine fed the cats, she grabbed her jacket off the Eastlake hall tree and went outside to sit on the front porch swing. She hadn't been sitting there long when Margie, who was working next door, spotted her and rushed over. Margie had won the bid to remodel the yellow brick foursquare next door to the mansion, which had been a speakeasy during Prohibition. She'd been juggling work between the two houses.

"Hey, kiddo," Margie called. "How did the first day go?"

"It was awful. Grab a seat and I'll tell you about it."

Margie sat down on one of the wicker chairs and said, "It can't be all that bad?"

"Way bad. As my Irish friend Colleen would say, 'Twas a nightmare to behold.' " Katherine proceeded to give Margie the short version of the morning gloom.

Margie said seriously, "I wonder why the massage queen would want to learn about computers?"

Katherine asked amused, "Does everyone in Erie call her that? Jake said the same thing."

Margie laughed. "I wouldn't worry about it. Listen, I've got to get back. I finally got sick of stripping that god-awful flowered wallpaper, so I hired a drywall crew to come in and re-do the walls." She started to get up, then abruptly sat back down.

Two pickup trucks pulled in front of the pink mansion and parked.

"Did you hire more workers?" Katherine asked.

"Kiddo, that's the Sanders bunch," Margie said nervously. She yanked out her cell and called Cokey, who was working next door as well. "Hey, Sugar Pop, I'm gonna leave my cell on. I'm on Katz's front porch. The Sanders boys just showed up. Might be trouble. I'll explain later. Tell the guys we might need them over here. I'll let you know." She placed the phone on her lap.

A man in his fifties with shoulder-length hair and a short-trimmed beard got out of one of the trucks. He went over to the passenger side and opened the door. Barbie leaped out. Four guys clambered out of the truck behind her.

Margie called from the front porch, "Howdy, Sam. How are you today?"

Sam took Barbie's arm and led her up to the porch. "Good afternoon, Ladies. Beautiful day. Are you Ms. Kendall, the teacher?" he asked pleasantly, without a hint of menace in his voice.

"Yes," Katherine said, not leaving the porch swing. "How can I help you?"

The four other men, ranging in ages from sixteen to thirty, stood on the concrete landing. The oldest had a buzz haircut with a long, shaggy beard. The younger one looked like a typical teenager, trying to keep up with the latest fashions. The other two could have been released from prison the previous day. One had dirty, long hair tied up in a ponytail, and the other had a mullet.

"I'm Sam Sanders. This is my daughter, Barbie. You two met earlier, and these are my sons. Meet Dave, my eldest," he said, pointing at the man with the buzz haircut. "And this here is Stevie and Bobby." Stevie with the ponytail raised his hand and glared, while Bobby with the mullet cackled nervously. "Not to forget my youngest son, Jerry." Jerry gave an insolent teenager's look. Sam continued, "We came over to offer our sincere apologies for what happened today. Barbie has something to say to you."

Barbie stood silent, looking very sullen. And only when prodded by her father did she speak. "I'm sorry," she said looking down at the porch floor. "I didn't mean all those ugly things I said to you."

Directly behind the porch swing, and inside the large picture window, the lace curtain parted to reveal two tall Siamese sitting on the windowsill. Scout and Abra surveyed the scene with hostile curiosity.

"Apology accepted," Katherine said.

"Oh, ha! Ha!" Barbie laughed loudly. "See Pop, I told ya we could fix it! When is the next class, Teach?"

Katherine looked shocked. "I'm sorry, but I've already scheduled another student to take your place. I'll have to place your application back in the candidate pool for the next session."

Sam drew his wallet out of his back pocket and extracted a hundred dollar bill. "Will this fix things?" he asked, flinging the money at Katherine.

Katherine thought fast on her feet and said with a winning smile, "Although your gratuity is quite nice, and your kind gesture is appreciated, I honestly cannot accept it."

From the corner of her eye, Katherine could see a group of men walking down the sidewalk, approaching the pink mansion from the yellow brick foursquare. She quickly glanced and observed Cokey leading the pack.

Katherine took the money and tried to hand it back to Sam, but he wouldn't accept it. "Look," she said firmly. "You better take it, because I'm not keeping it."

Sam's face clouded instantly. He yanked the money and stuffed it in his wallet.

Cokey called, "Hey, Margie and Katz, are you ready for a coffee break? The boys and I are headed to the Red Diner." Each one of *the boys* Cokey referred to resembled a pro wrestler.

Sam glanced irritably at Cokey. "We're just headin' out." He turned to leave, with Barbie close behind. Bobby tapped Barbie on the shoulder and said in a hushed tone, "Is that them?" He was eyeing the Siamese in the window.

"Oh, ha! Ha!" Barbie replied.

The Sanders bunch, including Barbie, got back in their trucks and left as speedily as they had arrived.

Overhearing the comment by the brother with the mullet, Katherine panicked. "I didn't like that remark about my cats. Barbie had asked me earlier if they were worth anything. Should I call Chief London?"

"Oh, hell no," Cokey answered. "You don't want to piss that bunch off. They're freakin' crazy."

"Thanks, love," Margie said looking affectionately at Cokey, "for rescuing us."

"Now, I meant it about coffee time; let's get in the truck and go. You ladies follow us," Cokey announced.

"I'm sorry, I'll have to take a rain check," Katherine apologized. "I've got a student coming soon."

Margie got up and said, "Call me if you need me, kiddo!" She left with the guys.

Katherine waved, and then went inside. Scout and Abra met her at the door. Both of them stretched up and wanted to be held. "That might be hard to do," she said, reaching down, lifting up both, and kissing them on their necks. When she set them back down, Scout emitted a nervous "Waugh."

"Don't worry, baby. I'm not going to let anyone hurt you."

Right as she was about to walk in the atrium, she heard a loud car pull up. Its muffler rivalled a sonic boom. She moved the front door side-panel to look. It was the replacement student. A young woman with long, dark hair parted down the middle was unbuckling a toddler from a car seat in her car. Katherine walked out to greet her.

"Hi, are you Stacy?" Katherine asked.

"Yes, I'm Stacy Grimes," the woman said as she picked up the child. "I've got a problem. My mom's sick and can't babysit. Can I come another time?" Her question came across as a plea.

"No problem. You can come right now. Your little girl is welcome, too."

"Oh, wonderful," Stacy said gratefully. "I have a portable playpen in the back of my car. If you could help me get it out, we can set it up."

"Okay, park in the back and I'll meet you at the back door."

"Super," Stacy started to put the little girl back in the car seat, but Katherine stopped her.

"Hey, I can hold her while you move the car."

"Oh, sure, thanks. Her name is Angelina," Stacy said, handing the toddler to Katherine.

Katz, who rarely held a baby, toddler or child, was a pro at cat handling. She cooed to Angelina in a soothing voice, and talked to her like she did to her cats, "Hey, sweetie, we're going to take a little walk."

The adorable child with curly black hair stuck her thumb in her mouth. While Stacy drove the car to the back, Katherine walked down the driveway behind her. They removed the playpen and assembled it in the classroom. Angelina was true to her name. She never cried and quietly played with her toys. After two hours, Stacy thanked Katherine several times. "I'm so glad for this opportunity. Someday, I want to move out of Erie and find a better-paying job."

Katherine smiled, and then observed a gold bracelet with a single charm on the little girl's left wrist, and commented, "That's a beautiful charm."

"Oh, thank you. I've got one, too," Stacy said proudly, holding up her arm. "Angelina's daddy gave it to us. He had 'angel' engraved on Angelina's and 'I Luv Mommy' on mine. After I drop Angelina off at my mom's house, I'm heading to see him."

Helping the young mother buckle Angelina in her car seat, Katherine said, "I'll see you on Wednesday for practice time." She waved as Stacy drove down the driveway.

Katherine thought, *If Stacy's mom is sick, why is she dropping Angelina off so she can go see the father? It doesn't make any sense*! Katherine shrugged her shoulders and stepped down into the classroom. Scout and Abra were sitting on her desk, sniffing the air.

"*That*, my furry little friends, was a baby girl," she said.

Scout started swaying back and forth. Abra began doing the same thing.

"What's wrong?" Katherine asked nervously. "Please don't do the Halloween dance."

"Raw," Abra shrieked. Scout was silent, but her pupils were mere slits in her deep blue eyes. Scout arched her back and began hopping up and down. Abra mimicked Scout's movements.

"Okay, you two. You're not in the Hocus Pocus show anymore. Cadabra, snap out of it!" she said, snapping her fingers. Cadabra was Scout's show name, but Katherine never called her that. She'd said it once before when Scout was in a trance and doing her Halloween dance, and it had worked. She hoped it would work this time as well.

Scout stopped and began licking behind Abra's ears. Abra closed her eyes and seemed to be in cat heaven.

Katherine moved over and petted them. "Scout, it really freaks me out when you do that dance. Bad things seem to follow. Now you've got Abra doing it too."

Scout licked her hand.

"Okay, the both of you are going back upstairs."

Without warning, Scout and Abra bolted out of the room and flew up the stairs to her office.

Suddenly, a strong premonition overcame Katherine. She sensed that Stacy was in some kind of danger, but she didn't know what kind. She shrugged it off as being just another bad vibe on a day that had not been one of her better days.

Chapter Three

Katherine was late getting up because one of the cats, probably Lilac, had pushed the alarm clock off the nightstand. Sometime during the night, the small, plastic clock had become a hockey puck. Katherine had readjusted her feather pillow, thinking she had plenty of time to snooze. But when the mid-morning sun filtered through the leaded glass transom and shot a bright beam on her forehead, she leaped out of bed. "Oh, my God! Jake is going to be here any minute and I'm not dressed." Katherine's sudden movement frightened Abby and Lilac, who darted off the bed and scrambled down the hall. Unfazed by the commotion, Scout and Abra were sitting on the dresser like bookends, but Iris was nowhere to be seen.

"Iris," Katherine called.

Iris sauntered into the room and yowled.

"Hey, Miss Siam, what have you been up to? Why didn't you wake me up?" She petted the Siamese on her back.

Katherine grabbed her cell off the charger and called Jake. He answered right away. "I got up late. I'm just getting ready now," she apologized.

Jake advised her to dress warmly and that he'd see her in thirty minutes.

Pressing the end button, she said to the cats, "I've got thirty minutes to feed you guys and get ready." Dashing into the bathroom, she quickly took a shower and washed her hair. She didn't waste time blow drying it because it was so short and would dry quickly anyway. She applied makeup and a hint of lip gloss. Racing into the bedroom, she put on her clothes. After she laced up her sneakers, she grabbed her cell and keys. Katherine flew down the hall and took the stairs at breakneck speed. The cats followed her, vocalizing their individual distinctive way. "Last one to the kitchen is a rotten egg," she said playfully to the cats. In record speed, she dished out food, then grabbed her bag and went to the front door to wait for Jake. Within a few seconds, he pulled up in his Jeep Wrangler. She dashed out and turned her key in the deadbolt lock on the front door.

Jake was walking up the sidewalk, holding a jacket. "Hey, it's really chilly out. You'll need more than the jacket you've got on. This is the coldest Covered Bridge I can remember." He handed her a beige field jacket.

Katherine took the coat and put it on. It obviously was one of Jake's, because it was way too big. She climbed into the Jeep and said excitedly, "Finally, I get to experience my very first Covered Bridge Festival."

Jake got in and answered, "There's several festivals going on at the same time, but we'll go to

the one in Millbridge. It's about an hour from here."
He started the Jeep, put it in gear, and drove out onto
Lincoln Street, making a U-turn.

They talked most of the way. That was one of
the reasons why Katherine liked Jake so much,
because it was easy to be around him. She had a gut
feeling that Jake felt the same way. She counted her
lucky stars.

"How's the party planning coming along?" he
asked, as he turned south onto U.S. 41. "I got my
invitation. Abra looks adorable in her purple cape.
Too bad you didn't include the pic you took of Scout
ripping it off," he kidded.

Katherine laughed. "You won't believe this, but
I hired a party planner."

"Really?" he asked. "That's cool."

"Michelle recommended her to me. So far, I'm
impressed. I've talked to her on the phone a few

times. She's hired a fortune teller to read fortunes and hold a séance in the attic."

"No way," Jake interjected.

"Way," she answered. "There'll be a close-up magician who'll find something that belongs to each guest, then hide it in the mansion. We'll be given maps. Whoever finds the most objects will receive a fifty dollar gift card."

"Sort of like a scavenger hunt?" Jake asked, amused. "But how does the magician find things on the guests?"

"Not sure. I'll have to ask the party planner."

"It might not be too safe for the magician to get too close to either Cokey or Daryl."

"Why?"

"Cokey and Daryl share more in common than the family name. They're also former marines. They might flip the magic man into next week."

Katherine laughed boisterously. "Flip him into next week. That's a good one."

"So what are we going to eat?" Jake asked.

"Typical man question," Katherine quipped. "Because the dining room table accommodates twelve people, I have invited twelve guests. Dinner will be catered by the Erie Hotel."

"Excellent!" Jake approved. "I hope prime rib is on the menu."

"For you, the world," Katherine said affectionately, then "Now, here's the coincidental part. The fortune teller and the magician are Russian, and both are from Brighton Beach, New York."

"Where's that?" Jake asked, slowing down for a squirrel that had darted across the road.

"Brighton Beach is located in lower Brooklyn. It's close to the famous Coney Island. It's full of immigrants from Russia. My mom and dad used to take me to their restaurants. Dad loved Russian food. We'd call a car service to drive us from Bay Ridge to Brighton."

"Fascinating," Jake said. "I've heard of Coney Island, but not Brighton or Bay Ridge."

"Maybe we could go there someday," Katherine suggested enthusiastically. "I can show you my old haunts."

"I'd love to," Jake said, then asked, "I take it your parents didn't own a car?"

"No need to. We had car services and the subway."

"I've been to New York, but never rode the subway."

"We'll have to fix that one day," she said, then changed the subject. "After I pick up Colleen from the airport on Friday, I'm meeting the party planner,

67

the fortune teller and the magician. We're going to do a dress rehearsal of the entertainment on Saturday."

Jake reached over and squeezed her hand. "It's going to be fun."

"Enough of my stuff. Tell me about Covered Bridge."

"It's sort of something you have to experience. The bridge in Millbridge is a reproduction, but a damn good one. Several years ago, some yahoo torched the original. It was devastating to the town because they base their livelihood on this once-a-year event. People were so disgusted by the arson, they took up donations. I'm talking statewide contributions. The town gathered enough money to build a brand-new bridge, which looks just like the original. That's the first thing you'll see when we pull in. You have to walk over it to get to the festival."

"Meaning no cars are allowed," she asked, interested.

"Just pedestrians," he said. "There's an actual mill that sells its own products. We'll have to pick up some of their pumpkin bread mix. It's delicious."

"I've never had pumpkin bread."

"Well, brace yourself, you'll have lots of pumpkin this and pumpkin that before the day is over."

"Wonderful," she said, enjoying gazing through the Jeep's window at the gorgeous autumn leaves. The sky was a deep blue without a cloud in sight.

Jake slowed down for an Amish horse-drawn vehicle that was moving at a snail's pace ahead. While he passed, Katherine smiled at the two women inside and turned back to Jake, "I didn't know there were any Amish in Indiana."

"Yes, there are. They own and farm land around here. They even have their own school for their kids. I bet the ladies are taking their produce to the festival," Jake observed. "Hopefully, there'll be pumpkin whoopies."

"I've had chocolate whoopies, but not pumpkin."

"They're basically round pumpkin cakes with a creamy cheese icing in the middle. You'll want to buy dozens and then take them home and freeze them. They're incredible."

"I'm salivating," Katherine replied with a smile.

Arriving at the festival, Jake parked the Jeep on a grass-covered parking spot. The lot was packed, so they had to hike quite a ways to get to the famous bridge. Katherine was in awe and quickly extracted her smartphone. She began taking pictures of the historic site. The crowd of people attending was vast, so it was impossible to get a clear shot of the bridge. A friendly passerby volunteered to take Jake's and Katherine's picture together. After thanking the photographer, Katherine told Jake she'd print a hard copy for him.

The setting was idyllic. The bridge crossed over a pond, complete with small waterfall. The small dam powered the mill, which was still in operation. As they walked over the covered bridge, Katherine began to notice "Wanted" posters stapled to the wood beams. She stopped and began to read one of them. "Information leading to the arrest of the Brook County killer who has murdered these young women . . . ," her voice trailed off. On the poster were photos of three beautiful women, each with long hair parted down the middle. They appeared to be in their early twenties.

"Oh, this is heartbreaking," Katherine said sadly.

Jake hugged her and said, "My cousin Daryl works for the sheriff's department. He said there's information about the killings that can't be made public. Daryl said whoever is committing the crimes is a sick bastard."

They started walking again. The throng of people had increased to the point it was hard to navigate the street. Festival goers pushed baby strollers, red wagons, or shopping carts. Families brought their children and their pets. A few attendees had their dogs in pet strollers. Katherine hoped viewing the poster wouldn't spoil her day. As a child, her mother would say, "Happy thoughts! Let it be!"

Jake took her hand and guided her to the mill. They toured the inside. Katherine was fascinated to watch the old equipment make flour. Outside, Jake found a bench and Katherine sat down. Jake said he'd be back in a minute. When he returned, he was carrying two cups of steaming spiced tea, along with a giant slice of pumpkin bread, topped with a huge dollop of whipped cream. The nearby picnic tables were packed with families talking and laughing. While Jake and Katherine ate, a fifty-something couple came over. The man was tall with dark brown hair and intense brown eyes. The woman was petite with shoulder-length graying hair. Jake recognized them immediately and stood up to offer his mom his seat.

"Hey, Mom and Dad," he said. "I didn't know you were coming today. Mom, have a sit-down next to Katherine."

"Thanks, son, but we just got here. I need to stretch my legs," she answered.

"Who's this young lady?" Jake's father asked, firing Katherine an inquisitive glance.

"Dad, this is Katherine," Jake said, with an ear-to-ear grin.

Jake's father extended his hand.

Katherine shook it heartily. "I'm so glad to finally meet you, Mr. Cokenberger."

"My name's Johnny."

Katherine smiled.

Johnny turned to the woman behind him and introduced her to Katherine. "And this is Jake's Mom, Cora."

Cora slowly stepped up to shake Katherine's hand, but never once established eye contact. "I'm pleased to meet you," she said in a monotone voice.

Katherine asked, smiling, "How are you enjoying the festival?"

Cora answered in a bored tone, "Just fine. John, I really want to go to the stained glass booth before they're all sold out."

"Sure thing," Johnny said, somewhat embarrassed by his wife's cold behavior toward Katherine. "Son, are you still stopping by later?"

"Yes, Dad, after I take Katz home."

"Okay, then. Nice meeting you, Katherine," Jake's dad said as he turned to leave.

Jake's face turned several shades of red. He looked at Katherine like he'd just experienced his worst nightmare. "Katz, I cannot apologize enough for my mother. I don't know why she acted that way."

Katherine was speechless. She felt hurt, no, crushed. She wanted so much for Jake's parents to like her. She just continued pretending to enjoy the pumpkin bread.

"I'm so sorry," Jake continued.

Katherine took Jake's face in her hands and kissed him lightly on the lips. "It's okay, really. Just let it be."

There was a dead silence for what seemed to be an eternity, but finally Jake changed the topic. "How did it go yesterday with the new student?"

"Good. Her name is Stacy. She had her adorable little girl with her. She said her mom was sick and she couldn't find a babysitter. So we hauled in the playpen, put Angelina in it, and I taught the class. It went by very smoothly. Stacy is a fast learner," Katherine answered, trying to be cheerful.

"What's her last name?" he asked.

"Grimes."

"I know her. She's a sweetheart. She's a server at the Erie Hotel. Ironically, she replaced . . . " Jake caught himself and fell silent.

Katherine thought, *Did the love of my life just almost mention that horrific Patricia Marston woman – the one who killed her mother, then my*

76

boyfriend? She answered gloomily, "I haven't been to the hotel in a long time."

"I'm sorry, Katz, it was insensitive of me to mention it," Jake apologized. Putting his arm around her, he said, "Forgive me?"

"I wonder if I can ever forget what happened last February," Katherine said sadly.

"What do you mean?" Jake asked, concerned.

"Until Patricia Marston is sentenced to life in prison, I won't have closure for Gary's death, but let's not talk about this now," Katherine said, quickly recovering. "By the way, why would you know Stacy? Should I be worried?" she asked warily.

Jake gave her an incredulous look. "Nope. After my wife died, I couldn't stand being home alone, so I frequented every bar and restaurant in town. That's how I seem to be the official social register of Erie. Stacy's had her share of tragedy.

Her father was killed in a hit-and-run accident. They never found out who did it. Her fiancé was a marine in Iraq, and then Afghanistan. He died in combat before they could marry."

Katherine looked puzzled. "What did you just say?"

"Which time?" Jake asked. "I seem to be babbling about negative stuff I really don't want to talk about."

"Go back to the part about Stacy's fiancé. He died in the war?"

Jake nodded. "What's so sad, he never got to see his little girl. He was overseas when she was born."

"Something doesn't gel. Yesterday when Stacy left the classroom, she said she was meeting the father of Angelina. Why would Stacy lie to me? I don't even know her," Katherine said, mystified.

Jake shrugged. "Don't know. There must have been a good reason though. Stacy's never come across as a liar." Jake got up and moved to the garbage can. He threw out the paper cups and plate. "Are you ready to see the sights?" he asked. "We'll just walk the streets. There are several historic buildings with vendors inside, and newer pole barns with folks selling just about anything. I know a vendor that sells flavored coffee. Want to go there first?" Jake said with renewed enthusiasm.

"Yes," Katherine said on autopilot. She was still wondering why Stacy lied.

Jake led the way through the crowd of people. "Does this remind you of Grand Central Station?" he kidded.

"Definitely, but the people dress very differently in Manhattan."

"But look at you," Jake said pointing at Katherine's field coat. "You fit right in!" He hugged her.

Jake and Katherine darted and meandered through a large group that included grandparents, parents and children to get to the coffee vendor. While Katherine bought several different flavors of coffee, Jake chatted to the vendor. Katherine liked that about him. He could strike up a conversation with anyone. A nearby country band played Hank Williams's "Your Cheatin' Heart." Not exactly Katherine's favorite song, considering her former boyfriends had all been cheaters, especially Gary.

Several hours passed. Jake and Katherine tried every pumpkin dessert at the festival – pumpkin ice cream, pumpkin roll with creamed cheese frosting, pumpkin whoopie pies, and a slice of pumpkin pie. For lunch they walked to the outdoor food court, which was packed. Most of the fare was food Katherine never imagined would be sold by vendors in Manhattan. Fried zucchini and green tomatoes, bloomin' onions with ranch dipping sauce, breaded pork tenderloin, chicken kabobs on a stick, and for dessert, cinnamon-sprinkled "elephant ears" and giant sticky buns with thick icing. Katherine and Jake explored them all, but jumped to the back of a long line for hickory-smoked chicken, which the vendor advertised as the best BBQ in Indiana. Later, they both agreed it was. Sitting at crowded picnic table and eating away, a tall slender man in his twenties walked over. He wore a county deputy uniform, complete with tasseled hat. He spoke to Jake.

"Hey, cousin," he said, flashing the Cokenberger grin. He had blond hair and light green eyes.

"Hey," Jake said, extending his hand. "Daryl, I want you to meet Katz."

Daryl bent down and kissed Katherine on the cheek. "The pleasure is all mine," he said.

Jake answered in a kidding tone, "Calm down there, Romeo."

Daryl belted out a laugh, sounding very much like Cokey.

Katz laughed. "It's nice to meet you. Jake has told me all about you. Did you get the invitation to my Halloween party?"

"Yes, I did, but if we don't catch this nutcase killing young women, I won't be able to attend. Sheriff's got us working around the clock."

"Oh, I'm sorry," Katherine said empathetically.

"Any new leads?" Jake asked.

The deputy waited for the family of teenagers to vacate the picnic table, then leaned over. He lowered his voice. "What I'm about to tell you is going to be released to the media in a couple of hours, but keep it to yourselves until you hear it on the news. We found another victim."

Katherine gasped, "Oh, no, that's so tragic."

"The weird thing is this psycho is profiling young women with the same hair style – long dark hair, parted down the middle."

"Sounds like Ted Bundy," Katherine commented.

"How do you know about Ted Bundy?" Jake asked, in passing.

"One of my electives at NYU was criminology. We studied serial killers. Ted Bundy preferred women with the same kind of hair style. Hope this killer isn't a copycat."

"Me either," the deputy agreed. "This attack is different from the rest. One of the state park employees found an abandoned car just outside the park entrance. The victim was abducted and discovered farther up the road. She was either thrown from a speeding vehicle or she managed to jump out. There were marks on her neck like someone tried to strangle her. She must have fought like hell. When an elderly couple came upon the scene, the perp sped off. They found the woman on the side of the road and called 9-1-1. She has some serious injuries, and it's not sure whether she'll make it or not. She was helicoptered to an Indianapolis hospital, where she's in a coma."

Jake asked, "Did the couple ID the make and model of the car?"

The deputy shook his head, "Nope, but they did say it had Indiana plates."

Katherine felt like she was going to faint. She remembered Scout and Abra doing the Halloween dance after Stacy and Angelina left the classroom. She asked, concerned, "Do you know the woman's name?"

Deputy Cokenberger shook his head. "We can't release the name until the family's been notified, but she's from Erie. Well, gotta get back to it. Nice meeting you, Katz. I do hope I can come to your party, but I'll let you know if I can't." He tipped his tasseled hat and walked through a crowd of people waiting in line for the fried green tomatoes.

"What's wrong, Katz? You look like you've seen a ghost."

"I don't have a very good feeling about this. Gut feeling tells me the woman is Stacy Grimes."

Katherine fished out her cell phone and pressed her contact's list. She scrolled through the names until she found Stacy's. She pressed the phone icon but the phone rang and rang, then went into voice mail. She left a message, then pressed the end button. "Stacy's not picking up. I'll use my phone app to find her mother's number." Searching the directory, Katherine asked Jake, "There's a million Grimes listed. Do you know Stacy's mom's name?"

"Nope," Jake said shaking his head. "I don't know Stacy's mom's name, but her deceased husband's name was Rick."

"Not finding it. Maybe it's not listed. I might have her mom's number on file in the classroom. I won't have a moment's peace until I find out Stacy's okay. Jake, can we go home now?" Katherine looked up with concern.

"Sure," Jake answered. "I'm completely pumpkined out anyway. Let's head to the Jeep."

They barely spoke on the way back to Erie. Jake tried his best to get Katherine to talk, but she just answered "yes" or "no" to his questions. Pulling up in front of the pink mansion, Jake said, "Do you want me to come in?"

Katherine touched his hand. "Yes, please do," she said. "Can you park in back?"

Jake backed up, then drove the Jeep to the classroom's entrance. They instantly noticed that the back metal security door was covered with oozing broken eggs.

"Oh, my God," she said loudly. "Who in the hell would do such a thing?"

Jake stopped the Jeep and they got out.

Jake said, "We've got to get this washed off before it dries and damages the paint. Could you unlock the door, please? I'll go inside and get a bucket of water and some soap. While I'm doing that, you can look for Stacy's mom's phone number. Sound like a plan?"

Katherine nodded and put her key in the lock. She opened the door and stepped down several steps. Jake walked back to the mechanical room's laundry sink and drew a pail of water. Katherine rummaged in her new desk and found the number for Stacy's mom; she added it to her smartphone's contact's list. A weak woman's voice answered the phone.

"Hello," the voice slurred.

Katherine wondered what drugs she might be on to cause such slurred speech. "Mrs. Grimes, this is Katherine Kendall. Stacy is taking a computer class from me . . ."

Mrs. Grimes interrupted, "Ma'am, Stacy won't be attending your class. She's in critical condition down in Indy. My sister is coming to drive me there."

"I'm so sorry. If there's anything you need, please don't hesitate to call me," Katherine said, worried.

"Thank you. I'm hanging up now. My ride is here." The distraught mother hung up.

"Jake," Katherine called urgently.

"What is it?" he said, dashing into the classroom with water splashing out of his bucket.

"The victim last night *was* Stacy. She's in critical condition in a hospital in Indy. I've got to call Chief London."

"Why are you calling the chief?" Jake asked, puzzled.

Katherine picked up her cell from the desk and called the chief. "Chief London, this is Katz Kendall. I think I have information regarding the Stacy Grimes case," she said, and then hesitated. "Yes, okay, pull up to the back of the house." She tucked her phone in her back pocket.

"Jake, the chief's going to be here any minute. I could have told him the info on the phone, but he insisted on coming over. Hand me a rag. That door is a mess!"

Both Jake and Katherine were busy washing the door when the chief drove up his cruiser and parked.

The chief got out and walked over. He immediately noticed the door.

"Damn kids," he said angrily. "Erie grocery stores aren't allowed to sell eggs to minors in October. I wonder how these brats are getting them. If it's any consolation, you're not the only folks in town getting egg-bombed."

Katherine rolled her eyes and said, "In Brooklyn we had a problem with spray paint, but can't remember if my parent's townhouse ever got egged."

"So, Ms. Kendall, how do you know Stacy Grimes?" the chief asked, coming right to the point. "It must be important, or you wouldn't have called."

"Stacy started my computer class yesterday. She brought her little girl because her mom was sick and couldn't babysit. Both Stacy and her little girl wore matching gold bracelets. When I admired them, Stacy said her daughter's father gave them the jewelry, and that they were meeting him in a few minutes," Katherine explained.

The chief wore his usual *hurry up and tell me* expression on his face.

Katherine took the hint and finished, "Then, Jake tells me the little girl's father died in combat overseas. So, why would she lie to me? Where was she going? Who was she meeting?"

The chief scratched his beard and said, "Thanks for the tip. I'll pass the info on to Sheriff Goodman. These multiple murders have everyone on edge, but this time the victim is from Erie. I pray Stacy makes it. She's the town's sweetheart, and everybody loves her. I've known her mom for a long time, and used to go fishing with her dad."

"Her mom said she was in critical condition, but I don't know the extent of her injuries," Katherine said sadly.

The chief said abruptly, "And you don't want to know, either. Keep this under your cap, but the doctors deliberately induced a coma so her body can heal. I believe in miracles. If Stacy makes it, I hope she can tell us who did this to her."

"Definitely," Katherine agreed.

Jake added, "We need to catch this sick son of a bitch before he strikes again."

"Exactly," the chief said, starting to leave. "Now, if you find out any intel about our 'eggers' let me know. I'm off duty now. The wife has a roast in the oven and if I don't get home soon, she'll be fit to be tied," the chief winked. He walked back to his cruiser, got in, and left.

Jake said, "Knowing the chief, I bet he's not going straight home."

"Why do you say that?"

"Because right about now he's heading for Indy to check on Stacy."

"But he said he was calling Sheriff Goodman," Katherine said, confused. "Is he the sheriff for Brook County?"

Jake nodded his head. "Oh, the chief will call him. Just sayin.'" Jake threw the rag into the bucket. "We're done here. Margie will be happy she won't have to repaint the door."

"I'm going inside to feed the cats," Katherine said, leaving.

"While you're doing that, I'm going next door to see if your neighbor saw anything."

"Not too likely," Katherine said. "Mrs. Harper is in poor health, but you might want to ask the home health aide. She may have seen something."

While Jake walked next door, Katherine locked the exterior classroom door. She headed toward the carport side of the mansion. The overhead porch had been heavily damaged by the tornado. Reconstruction had been very labor intensive and involved lots of millwork. The building was finally finished, and Margie was beginning her four-color-scheme paint work. Two levels of scaffolding still remained.

Katherine shifted her eyes to the three new double-hung kitchen windows that Cokey and Jake had installed. She saw two cats per window: Abra and Scout were in the first one, followed by Lilac and Abby in the middle, and a lonely Iris in the third. On the inside, Cokey had widened the window sills to give the cats more room, making it easier for them to bask in the sun. The cats were clearly agitated, so she ran to the side steps, hurriedly put the key in the lock, and rushed inside. The cats were caterwauling loudly. The kitchen was a complete disaster. All the cabinet doors were open, and numerous dishes had been knocked out.

94

They were lying on the ceramic tile floor, broken into bits.

Jake walked in, "What the hell!" he said.

Katherine grabbed the closest cat and began checking for injuries. Jake did the same. Judging by the number of broken pottery shards, Katherine was shocked that none of the cats was seriously wounded. Jake and Katherine grabbed two at a time and put them in a different room. Iris was yowling at the top of her lungs. Katherine snatched her around the middle.

"Shhh, Miss Siam," Katherine cooed. "Was it you, Fredo? Did you do this?"

"Yowl," Iris bellowed in protest.

While Katherine consoled the upset Siamese, Jake found a broom and dustpan and began cleaning up the mess. He said, "You seriously think one of the cats did this?"

"Well, unless the pink mansion has a poltergeist!" Katherine replied, putting Iris in with the other cats. Scout tried to lunge out. "Not happening, magic cat!" She closed the door and said, "Iris likes to open the cabinet doors. Maybe she opened them and another cat pushed the dishes out."

"But why just the dishes?"

Katherine shrugged.

"We'd better childproof the cabs," Jake offered, as he finished sweeping up the mess.

"Something really upset them. They were all hyper when I came in."

"They probably saw whoever threw the eggs and it scared them," Jake suggested.

"Did you find out anything next door?"

"Nope. Mrs. Harper didn't see a thing, but she's in a wheelchair. Unless she was parked by one of the windows facing the mansion, she wouldn't have seen anything anyway. The health aide said she'd taken Mrs. Harper to a doctor's appointment, so whoever threw the eggs could have done it then. Probably like the chief said – a bunch of Erie brats having some pre-Halloween fun."

"Or it could have been Barbie Sanders," Katherine added.

"Not thinking so," Jake said skeptically. "Katz, I promised my dad I'd come over so I'd better take off. Do you want to help me unload the Jeep? I think you bought everything for sale at the festival. But first," he said, taking Katherine into his arms. "I want to thank you for a wonderful day. Let's make this a tradition." He kissed her on the forehead.

Katherine said, "I'm game."

*   *   *

A few minutes after Jake left, Katherine was heading for the atrium to go upstairs when the front

97

doorbell clanged noisily. She rushed to open it. Margie was standing outside, holding a box.

"Come in," Katherine said smiling, holding the door open.

"Hey, kiddo. The oops man left this by accident at the yellow brick house."

"Oh, yay! I was worried it wouldn't come. Just set it down any old place."

Margie put the large box on the atrium floor.

"Why do you call the delivery guy the oops man?" Katherine asked curiously.

"Because he's always delivering to the wrong address. The joke is he's been doing this run for twenty years, but I think he's developed cataracts. He's a good soul, so nobody complains. I've got a box cutter. Want me to open it?" Margie offered.

"Yes, please. And, thanks for bringing it over."

Margie slit the tape and tugged the box open. Inside were more Halloween decorations, with a twelve piece serving set of black dishes, cups and saucers.

Katherine clapped. She carefully removed the carton of dishes and opened it. Examining the plate, she handed it to Margie. "I thought it was cool the way it has a cobweb design etched in white."

"Rather ghoulish!" Margie laughed.

"I'll have to eat off these dishes for a while," Katherine lamented.

"Why's that?" Margie asked.

"My cats opened the cabinet with the dinner plates and hurled them out. Once they hit the ceramic floor, they broke into smithereens."

"Eek!" Margie grimaced. "Spitfire has never done anything like that."

"They were expensive, too. Tiffany. Waterford."

Margie asked, "Were they antiques?"

"No, they're new patterns. When I moved here, I thought it was strange that practically everything in the house was brand new, from the dinnerware to the cleaning equipment. It's like the housekeeper had a field day buying new stuff. Or my great aunt did. It's a mystery," Katherine said, throwing her hands up. "I'll just add the broken dishes to the growing list of cat disasters. My dear estate lawyer asked me to keep track."

"I hope it's a short list," Margie teased.

"Sort of," Katherine smirked.

Margie chuckled. "It won't be too long before you don't have to put up with him. What is it? Five months?" Margie asked.

Katherine answered, "Four months. I'll replace them, or try. Or not. In a few months a few broken dishes won't matter. I'll buy whatever I want."

Margie said, "I better get going. I need to grab a few things at the brick house, then head on home to start dinner. I gave strict orders to Tommy and Shelly to not open the door to anyone unless it's me or their dad. This psycho running loose on a murder spree has everyone on edge."

"I met Deputy Daryl today at the festival. He talked a little bit about it. Oh, and I finally met Jake's mom and dad."

"Interesting." Margie gave an understanding, knowing look. "How did that go?"

Katherine threw her head back and laughed. "My worst nightmare. Jake's dad seems really nice, but his mom was as cold as ice."

Margie said, "It can't be as bad as that. Cora takes some getting used to. I've lived next door to her for years, and we still ain't friends. She was like that in high school. Got her nose stuck up so high, I'm surprised she doesn't fall over backwards."

Katherine appreciated the moral support. "These facts are good to know."

"Okay, kiddo. Gotta go. Take care now." Margie left. Katherine shut the door behind her and locked it. She picked up the box and hauled it to the kitchen, where she placed it on the Parsons glass-top aluminum table. Scout and Abra appeared out of nowhere and offered their help.

"Not happening," Katherine said to the inquisitive cats. "I need to hide these so you pesky cats don't break them, because if you do, my guests will be eating off paper."

"Raw," Abra cried, fishing out a roll of black crepe paper. She clamped her jaw on it and bounced off the table with Scout in hot pursuit.

Katherine sat down and laughed heartily. It helped reduce her tension and anxiety about the events of the day. She then got up to look for the Siamese. She found them in the dining room, unravelling the roll and streaming it across the floor.

"Okay, let me have it. I'm going to decorate for the party. You two go find something else to do."

Scout and Abra sassed loudly as they scampered out of the room to pursue other feline adventures somewhere else in the house.

*   *   *

On Wednesday, an hour before the students would arrive for their computer skills practice session, Katherine was rummaging in the carriage house for a rake. She rarely ventured inside the restored building, because the space was completely packed with what she called junk, ranging from the old metal corrugated roofing panels stacked in a corner, to an ancient-looking golf cart. Someday, when the house was legally hers, Katherine planned to have the inside converted into a garage, so she could park her new Subaru.

Today, she noticed for the first time, a tall wooden ladder leading to an area she hadn't explored. Carefully climbing the rungs to the ceiling, she pushed a trap door open and gazed into the entire upper expanse of the carriage house, where hay might have been stored long ago. It was littered to the ceiling with more junk. Not relishing opening a can of "cleaning worms" as she had when she cleaned the basement, she made a mental note to pursue it later.

While climbing down the ladder, she didn't hear a vehicle pull up, nor see the two men who walked inside. Four feet from the bottom of the ladder, a rung snapped, sending Katherine into a free fall. One of the men caught her in his muscular arms. It was one of the Sanders boys. Unfortunately, it was the one who looked like he'd just been released from prison. The only difference in appearance was he seemed to have washed his hair, but it was still tucked back into a ponytail. The second brother wore a mullet. He cackled nervously.

"Be careful there, ma'am," he said, setting her down. "That ladder ain't no good."

Katherine caught her breath and said, "Thanks. What can I do for you today?" She backed up and inched her way to the door.

"We met you the other day. I'm Stevie Sanders, and this is my numb-nuts brother, Bobby."

"I ain't a numb-nut!" Bobby objected.

Stevie ran his eyes over Katherine, up and down in a suggestive manner. "What can you do for me today?" he said in a sexy voice.

Katherine walked out and headed for the classroom.

Stevie caught up with her, "Hey, Lady, I didn't mean to piss you off. I've come to haul the scrap metal away."

It was then that Katherine realized two pickup trucks were parked in back. Two other tough-looking men sat inside one. She said cautiously to Stevie, "I don't own this house. You'll have to talk to Mark Dunn."

"No need to bring a lawyer in it," he said indifferently. "Can I talk to the old lady that lives here?"

"My great aunt Orvenia passed away last winter."

"I'm sorry, ma'am. She gave me a note," he said, tugging a torn piece of paper from his denim pocket. "She gave me the metal in exchange for putting on a new roof. I had to do some work . . . some time for the state, so I wasn't able to git here right away."

Katherine made the connection between the word "state" and prison. She looked at the note. From seeing her great aunt's signature on various documents, she could confirm it was her handwriting.

Katherine shook her head. "I can't help you here. I don't have the authority to allow anything to be removed from this carriage house. Let me call Mark Dunn."

"We don't want any trouble, ma'am," Stevie said with narrowed eyes. "We came to git what belongs to us."

Katherine extracted her phone and called Mark Dunn. He wasn't in his office, so she left an urgent voice mail.

"As you could hear," she began. "I called Mark. He's the lawyer for my great aunt's estate. If you'd give me your number, I'll have him call you."

Bobby continued his nervous cackling, which now sounded like a hyena.

Stevie threw Katherine a menacing look and stormed to his truck, with Bobby close behind. The other truck pulled out first, and then Stevie peeled out. He yelled out the window, "We'll be back!"

Great, Katherine thought. *Nothing like alienating the Sanders family any more than I've already done.*

Chapter Four

Katherine arrived at the Indianapolis airport and parked in the cell phone lot. Within a few seconds, Colleen called and said her flight had arrived early, and she'd already picked up her bags. Katherine couldn't believe her good timing. She started up the engine, headed back onto the service road, and drove to the airline's arrival area. Colleen was waiting outside near the curb; her long red hair enveloped her face. It was a typical blustery fall day. Katherine temporarily parked the Subaru and got out to help Colleen with her bags.

"Katz," Colleen said. "Give me a hug. It is so wonderful to see you."

Katherine hugged her back. "You look great. Where's Jacky?" she asked, looking around.

"Jacky couldn't come. There was some last-minute emergency. His super was in a motorcycle accident and broke his arm. Jacky will have to do double-duty. He's really disappointed."

"Oh, no. I so much wanted him to come!"

"Maybe he can change his ticket and come out later when his boss is better."

"Let me help you with your bags," Katherine said, opening the back hatch.

"Wow, now this is a vehicle," Colleen praised. "It's certainly a far cry better than the ancient Toyota."

Katherine laughed. "I miss that car. But I love this one, though. Jake named her Sue-bee. Indiana guys have a thing with naming things."

Colleen smirked. "That's rich."

Katherine and Colleen both picked up Colleen's large suitcase and hoisted it in the back.

"It's a bit heavy," Colleen apologized.

"You think?" Katherine teased.

"I brought my spirit hunting equipment. Well, not all of it. I didn't want to chance the more expensive stuff getting broken," she said tongue-in-cheek, referring to her ghost meter, which was destroyed by Frank and Beatrice Baker when they vandalized her room during her last visit.

Katherine closed the hatch. Colleen got in and Katherine climbed in behind the wheel.

"Are you hungry? We could stop to get a bite to eat." Katherine checked the mirror, then merged into traffic.

"I'm famished," Colleen complained.

"Remember that restaurant we went to in Ohio – Down Home Cookin'? There's one several miles from here."

"I love that place! Yes, by all means."

On the way to the restaurant, Colleen talked about her cab drive from Manhattan to LaGuardia.

"'Twas a nightmare to behold," she began. "The cabby kept looking at me in his mirror. I screamed several times, or we'd all be killed."

Arriving at the restaurant, Katherine lamented that most of the parking spaces were taken, but found one behind the back dumpster. "I have rotten luck with parking spaces."

The two friends walked in and a friendly hostess seated them in front of a blazing fireplace. They both chose the special with sweetened ice tea.

Colleen asked, "Tell me about the party? I can't wait."

Katherine filled her in while they waited for their food. "I hired a party planner. For Halloween parties, she uses a Russian act from Brighton Beach. Supposedly, they're originally from Moscow. The fortune teller does various readings, and the magician does close-up magic."

"Brighton Beach, Brooklyn? No way. That's really close to where you grew up. What are they doing out here?"

Katherine shrugged, then continued, "When the guests arrive, we'll have cocktails and hors d'oeuvres, then sit down in the formal dining room for dinner. The Erie Hotel is catering it."

"The mention of that hotel always makes me remember poppy seeds, Patricia and poison," Colleen spitted with a wry smile.

Katherine didn't comment, but said, "After dinner, we'll gather in the attic for a séance or game of Ouija board."

"Not so keen on the Ouija board, Katz," Colleen said seriously.

"Why?" Katherine asked, surprised.

"You could easily conjure up a bad spirit. My paranormal group doesn't recommend it. The Ouija board opens up a portal and evil can get in."

"But it's just for fun."

"Not a good idea, trust me. Would your party planner get into a snit if I offered a suggestion?"

"I'm paying her, so it's my call," Katherine said.

"We could decorate the attic with spooky stuff, then go up for a spirit hunting session. I have my EMF meter, which you're familiar with."

"The needle flips to red when there's a ghost," Katherine remembered.

"Uh-huh. I also brought a digital voice recorder to record EVPs . . ."

"What's that?" Katherine asked.

"EVP is short for 'Electronic Voice Phenomena,' which records spirit voices not audible to the human ear."

"Oh, that's creepy as hell. I'd move out of the house if it picked up my great aunt or bootlegging great uncle complaining about something," Katherine announced.

"I also brought my pen-style digital infrared thermometer. It checks for cold spots in the house."

"Last winter just about every part of the house had a cold spot," Katherine joked.

"You said last spring you had a paranormal encounter with cold air wafting by you. The thermometer would pick that up."

"I hate to be the bearer of bad news, but that's the room you'll be staying in. You don't mind sharing it with a ghost, do you?" Katherine said facetiously.

"Cool," Colleen said with a grin.

"Oh, and by the way, you've really become sophisticated with this, Colleen. I'm impressed, but I'm having second thoughts about the attic ghost hunting idea. Can I take that idea under advisement?"

"You sound like Mark Dunn."

"I think it's in bad taste so soon after several people were murdered in my house. I don't want the Erie folk's tongues a-flappin.'"

"Tongues a-flappin'? You're starting to talk like the natives."

"The natives in Indiana are called Hoosiers," Katherine kidded.

The server brought over their country fried chicken dinner with white gravy, along with mashed potatoes, green beans, and coleslaw. She set down two tall glasses of sweetened iced tea.

"Oh, I love their food," Colleen said, diving in. "Tell me more about Jake. I know he looks like Johnny Depp, he loves cats, and they love him too. You said he's polite, sweet, caring . . . But what are you *not* telling me, girlfriend to girlfriend?"

Katherine put her fork down and sighed, "He's so wonderful. I'm just waiting for him to mess up."

"Like Mario did," Colleen said icily. "You'd think he'd at least text and let me know he got to Italy okay. I haven't heard one word from him. He doesn't return my emails. He hasn't called me. He dumped me – plain and simple!"

"Did you have a clue he was going to quit his job and move to Italy?" Katherine asked sympathetically.

"Woman's intuition, I guess," Colleen answered. "Mario always had a roving eye. I mean, when we'd go out to dinner, I'd try my best to look gorgeous for him, but I'd catch him looking at other women. If a server was good looking, he'd chat her up. It made me livid."

"Gary did the same, but he was a serial cheater. I knew Mario as the polite doorman, so I never knew how he acted outside the job. When I was there St. Patrick's Day, I noticed he was somewhat aloof, but I just assumed he was in a mood."

"So, Katz, I'm moving on. I had my crying spell, and now I'm ready to start again."

"Hear! Hear!" Katherine said, raising her iced tea glass for a toast. "May Colleen find the man of her dreams."

Colleen said with a grin, "May Katz find the perfect man who isn't allergic to cats."

"You'll meet Jake this evening." Katherine winked. "He's taking us to a fish fry. Covered Bridge Festival, which you missed, is in its final death throes of killing everyone with pumpkins.

Jake said the fish fry is the last event and is being held at the Erie fire station."

"Did you say 'fire station'?" Colleen asked, suddenly perking up to the idea of meeting a handsome fireman.

Katherine read her friend's mind, "I'm sure at least one of the firemen will pass your inspection. Jake's going to pick us up at six."

"Perfect! Can't wait to meet him. Have you met his parents yet?" Colleen asked, in-between bites of green beans.

Katherine made a face. "Ah, I met them yesterday at Millbridge. It was at one of the Covered Bridge Festivals; Jake took me."

"Let me guess. Dad looks like Johnny Depp senior, and mom looks like a movie star."

Katherine grimaced. "Yes, Jake's dad did look like Johnny Depp senior, but mom was a different story. Envision a pinched-faced plain Jane. Also, one that's as friendly as a rattlesnake."

"Shut the door! No way!" Colleen said, shocked.

"Way," Katherine answered. "She gave me the cold shoulder for reasons unexplained."

"Strange. You're so bubbly. Why would she do that?"

Katherine shook her head. "Maybe she thinks I'm a gold digger, after her son's money."

Colleen cleared her throat dramatically and reminded, "*You're* the one getting the big bucks."

"Or maybe she thinks Jake's seeing me too soon after his wife died. I'm committing some kind of Erie taboo by dating her son."

"Wow, Katz. You might have something there. Hasn't it been a year?" Colleen asked.

"Yes," Katherine answered.

"Maybe Jake's mom doesn't think that's long enough."

"I'm not going to worry about it," Katherine said. "How about we settle up and hit the road? I've got an appointment later with the party planner."

*   *   *

When Katherine and Colleen drove up in front of the pink mansion, the driveway was blocked by a large Four Winds motorhome with a New York license plate: *13 Magic.*

Colleen chuckled, "Must be the magician."

"Yes, a magic man who doesn't know how to park," Katherine complained. A red Mini Cooper was parked in front of the motorhome. "That must be the party planner, but they're early." She pulled the Subaru in front of the Mini, turned off the ignition, and hopped out. A woman in her late forties with pancake makeup, fake eyelashes, and a crop of short purple hair met her on the sidewalk.

The passenger – a heavy-set woman with red hennaed hair – climbed out after her. Colleen began collecting her luggage to take inside.

"Are you Katherine Kendall?" the purple-haired woman asked.

Katherine smiled. "Are you Mary?"

"Yes, I'm so glad to meet you. I'm so sorry we're early, but Misha, the magician, got the time confused. He called me from the road, so I picked up Bella and practically flew to Erie."

A short, stocky man with wavy black hair and a large mustache, dressed in a black leather jacket, red sateen shirt and blue jeans, climbed out of the motorhome. He hurried over to the women and spoke in a sultry Russian accent, "Are you Carol?" he asked Katherine.

"My name is Katherine. You can call me Katz."

He ceremoniously took Katherine's hand and kissed it. Katherine quickly withdrew her hand for fear of what else the man might do. "Katsee, my name is Misha," he said.

"Pleased to meet you."

"Katz, this is Bella," Mary introduced. "Bella and Misha are originally from Moscow, but moved to Brooklyn several years ago."

Bella smiled, revealing a set of gold-capped teeth. "Da, Katsee, we much like you house." Her accent was thicker than the magician's.

When Colleen got out, Misha ran over to her side of the car, but Colleen dodged him with her carry-on bag. "Katz, I'm going in," she announced. "Can you lock the car? We can come back later for the suitcase."

"Nyet!" Misha said to Colleen, eyeing her up and down. "I carry."

"Okay," Colleen said. She whispered to Katherine, who was standing close by. "Is he a dead ringer for Boris Badenov, or what? *You* know, 'Moose and Squirrel.'"

"Stop it. He'll hear you," Katherine whispered, amused. She opened the Subaru hatch and Misha hoisted the heavy suitcase out.

Katherine guided the group to the front porch and opened the door. "Please come in," she said. Colleen made a dash for the back of the house. "Let's sit in the parlor." Katherine pointed the way. Katherine, Bella and Mary sat down, but Misha remained standing.

Mary said, "We'll go over the plan for the party – a quick overview. Bella, would you like to start?"

Bella was too preoccupied to answer. She was staring with eyes wide open at the two felines sitting on top of the wood window valance. "I h-h-hate kats," she slurred, then sneezed.

Katherine threw her a dirty look. "And?" she asked defensively.

"I von't *vork* with *k-k-kat.*"

"Mary, can I have a word?" Katherine got up and led Mary into the atrium. She said in a lowered voice, "My house is full of cats."

Mary said with sudden energy. "Bella barely speaks English. She meant to say she's allergic to cats."

As if on cue, Bella sneezed again in the next room.

Abby and Lilac looked down with feline disdain for the humans invading their territory.

"Okay, fine, but I plan on locking up the cats when the party takes place. I'll make sure the parlor is super clean so she won't have an allergy attack."

"Cool," Mary said, walking back into the parlor.

Misha was eyeing the cloisonné collection that filled a glass-front cabinet. "Katsee, would you like to make a *bizz*-ness? I buy," he said pointing at the vases.

"No," Katherine said abruptly. "Can we begin the meeting?" She was getting a headache from being called the wrong name.

Mary began, "You mentioned in your email there'll be cocktails before the dinner. I suggest Bella read fortunes first. This room will be perfect for that. She likes to do readings individually."

Colleen returned to the front of the house and came into the parlor. "Hello! I'm Colleen," she declared, then asked Bella, "Do you use a crystal ball or read palms?"

Misha said to Bella something in Russian. "Da," Bella answered. "Krystal ball and Kards."

"Tarot cards?" Colleen asked further.

126

Misha said, "Da."

Mary explained. "While the cocktails are served, Misha will be mingling with the guests. He'll perform several tricks, then take something from each person. When he's finished, he'll give them to me and I'll draw a scavenger's hunt map. Katz, does your printer have a copy feature?"

Katherine answered, "Yes, of course. But can you clarify how Misha takes something from each person?"

Misha laughed with a deep bellow. "I take *somezink* from you." He drew out of his jacket pocket Katherine's cell phone.

"I'll take that," Katherine said quickly, snatching it. "That's amazing," she said, returning the cell to her back pocket. "I was pickpocketed and I didn't even know it."

"Katsee, it's magic," Misha said, taking a dramatic bow.

Iris marched into the room with her tail hiked up. She eyed the group suspiciously, then trotted over to the Russian magician. "Yowl," she cried sweetly, collapsing on the man's leg.

"Iris," Katherine said, moving rapidly to pick her up, but Misha beat her to the punch.

The magician reached down, scooped Iris up, and cradled her in his arms. He then started cooing something in Russian to the seal-point Siamese, who seemed to be in a state of pure catly ecstasy. With eyes crossed, Iris began purring loudly.

Katherine said worriedly, "Oh, please let me have her." The Russian kissed Iris on the nose, cooed something else in Russian, and then handed her to Katherine.

Katherine held Iris close. "Excuse me. I'll be right back," she said. She walked to her back office area and gently scolded Iris. "You're not supposed to do that with strangers. What if he tried to hurt you?" Iris gave Katherine a haughty look, and then let out a barrage of loud 'yowls.'

"A little less conversation," Katherine said, locking the sassy cat in the powder room.

Returning to the parlor, Katherine said to Mary, "I don't know how my guests will feel about being pickpocketed. I think I should warn them in advance so if someone doesn't want to participate, they'll be exempted from the act."

Mary agreed, "Sure thing. Now while you're having dinner, Misha and I will place each personal item in an envelope with the owner's name. Then I'll seal it and assign a number, which will coincide with an approximate hiding place on the map. I'll use your printer to copy the map for each guest. After I hide the items, we'll take our leave."

"Sounds fine to me," Katherine said. "Just make sure I have the maps."

Mary continued, "Definitely! So, I'll expect payment before dinner. Bella and Misha prefer cash. Would that be a problem?"

"Cash it will be."

"You're going to have a wonderful party," Mary said excitedly, running her hand through her hair.

Colleen, who had been quietly listening, spoke up, "How long will the scavenger hunt take?"

Mary spoke animatedly. "I'd guess-timate about two hours. Generally, when there are twelve guests, each search takes ten minutes, give-or-take."

Katherine said to Colleen, "I could call intermission mid-way and serve dessert."

"Cool," Colleen said.

Misha stood in the atrium and was eying a crystal Tiffany wine decanter with matching goblets. He called to Katherine, "Wanna make a *bizz*-ness? How much dollars?"

"No, again," Katherine said, then to Mary. "Another word," she led Mary to the dining room. She said firmly, "How much do you know about this man? Misha's been casing the joint ever since he walked in."

"Oh, I assure you. They are honest people. They've worked for me for two years now. I've never had a complaint or had anything stolen."

"Good to know. Listen, I think this wraps things up," Katherine said hastily. "I'll call –"

She was interrupted by Bella shouting from the parlor. "A v-v-vat," the fortune teller screamed. When Colleen saw what "a vat" was, she darted to the back of the house.

Katherine, Mary and Misha ran into the parlor. "What's wrong?" Katherine asked, then observed Scout by the fireplace with her paw pressed down on a squirming black creature. "Waugh!" Scout cried happily, with a delicious twinkle in her blue eyes.

Abra stood nearby. Her whip-like tail was flicking back and forth in a state of feline excitement. The Siamese looked up at Katherine with curious expressions on their brown masks as if to ask, "Why are you bothering us? We're having fun here."

"Scout, let that bat go!" Katherine ordered.

Mary ran into the living room. "A bat!" she yelled. Bella grabbed her capacious gypsy bag and fled the scene, slamming the front door behind her. Through the parlor window, Katherine watched her half-running, half-waddling to the party planner's red Mini Cooper.

Mary returned to the parlor and stood uneasily, half-behind Katherine.

"Katsee, I get," Misha volunteered. He removed his leather jacket and moved toward Scout. Scout lifted her paw and the bat flew up and seemed to bounce off the wall. Abby and Lilac remained on the valance and were taking swipes at the bat as it flew by. Scout and Abra began springing in the air like ballerinas, trying to snatch the flying creature.

Misha got too close to the pair. Abra hissed a ferocious warning at the Russian.

"Nice, kitty katsee," Misha implored. The bat flew around the room, darting here and there, skirting Mary's hair, which sent the party planner into another screaming frenzy.

"Misha, don't let the bat bite you," Katherine warned.

Finally, Misha scooped the bat in his jacket. He ran outside and let the bat go.

Scout tried to run outside and do further chase, but Katherine tackled her near the door. "Not so fast, magic cat. We're going to join Iris in the next room."

Mary grasped her bag and went to the door. "Katz, I'll call you later." She hurriedly left.

Still clutching Scout, Katherine shut and locked the front door. "Waugh," Scout protested, kicking her.

"Okay, okay!" When she set her down, Abra trotted over and boxed Scout between the ears. "Raw," she cried in a tone that seemed to scold her sister for trying to escape.

"Well, cats, that's one way to clear a room," Katherine teased. "Let's go find Colleen." She then headed to the back of the house with Scout and Abra tagging along behind her. When she let Iris out of the powder room, Scout and Abra chased the sassy Siamese to the kitchen, where Katz found Colleen laughing hysterically. She had dropped into a modern aluminum side chair. Her head was tipped back and she was fanning herself with her hand. "That was hilarious!" Colleen uttered between giggles. "I watched it from the back hallway door."

Katherine rolled her eyes. "Well, carrot top. You know where the bat came from, right?"

"No, where?"

"No matter how many different locks I've had installed on the attic door, Scout figures it out and opens it. Do you still want to do your ghost hunting gig up there?"

"It's called spirit hunting," Colleen said, then added, "If there's bats up there, maybe we can find another place."

Katherine extracted her cell out of her pocket and called the vet. The receptionist Valerie answered. Katherine explained the situation. While she waited for Dr. Sonny to come to the line, she said to Colleen, "Scout could have been bitten by that poor creature."

"But she's had her shots, right?" Colleen asked, suddenly no longer amused, but worried about Scout.

"Yes, she's up-to-date on her shots, especially the rabies one. Bats carry rabies, you know."

"Saw it on Animal Planet," Colleen commented.

Katherine remembered how Colleen seemed to see *everything* on Animal Planet. "Are you addicted to that channel?" she asked.

"Guilty!" Colleen confessed.

Dr. Sonny came on the line and Katherine told him about Scout's bat adventure. Since the bat hadn't been caught for analysis, and might have been positive for rabies, he suggested that Katherine bring the cats to the clinic for thorough examinations. He then asked if any of the guests had been bitten.

"No, we were too busy running around and screaming to be bitten. I'm sure the bat was scared to death. Thank you so much, Dr. Sonny. I'll bring my kids in right away." She ended the call.

"Ma-waugh," Scout disagreed and fled to the center of the house. This initiated a feline steeplechase race with Scout in the lead, Abra a close second, and Iris bringing up the rear. Katherine and Colleen burst out laughing as they heard the cats thundering up the stairs and then racing to the back of the house.

Chapter Five

Katherine sat at her computer in the back office. Checking her emails, she was delighted that everyone invited to the party, except Jacky, would be attending. For the first time in a long time, she felt excited and happy. Colleen came into the room, with Scout and Abra following. They darted in and out of Colleen's path like porpoises in front of a moving ship.

"Katz, they're truly trying to kill me," Colleen complained. "I can hardly walk in my new shoes."

With the mention of shoes, Katherine turned around and looked. Colleen was wearing a pair of hot pink, pointy toe, four-inch heel pumps. Not wanting to hurt her friend's feelings, Katherine said sweetly, "The shoes are to die for, but carrot top, no one in Erie wears stiletto heels to a fish fry."

"Oh," Colleen blushed. "I guess that would be an Erie fashion *faux pas*!"

"Did you bring running shoes? I wear mine all the time," Katherine suggested.

"Yes, of course. I'll go up later and change. How about a bit of tea?" Colleen suggested, moving to the kitchen.

"Great. Let me save my document, and I'll be right there."

Colleen walked into the kitchen and gasped, "Katz, the cabinet doors are open!"

Katherine joined her and stifled a laugh. "The pink mansion has a poltergeist." Then her face clouded when she remembered two similar events.

Colleen noticed the change of expression and asked, "Katz, what's wrong?"

"Deja vu! Iris did this little cabinet door trick the very last time Carol Lombard visited, and right before she died in the fatal car accident." Katherine leaned against the counter. "After I learned my student, Stacy, was brutally assaulted, I came home to find not only the cabinet doors open, but broken dishes scattered on the floor."

Colleen tried to make light of the tense situation. "Are the cups broken, too? Should I look for Styrofoam cups for tea?"

"Either Iris did it, or the mansion really does have a poltergeist," Katherine said, trying to regain her good mood.

"Eerie!" Colleen said. "Maybe I should go get the EVP to detect if a spirit is trying to communicate. It would take a tremendous amount of ghostly energy to open those doors."

Abby chased Lilac into the kitchen. Lilac meyowled loudly, sprang from the ceramic tile floor to the granite counter, to the top of the cabinets, then raced their full length. From the cabinets, she leaped onto the wood window valance and ran across it. Right before the edge, she flopped on her side.

Abby did the same, except Abby flopped down the other way. They looked like a vintage ceramic cat lamp. "Chirp," Abby announced proudly.

Colleen took her smartphone and snapped a pic of the two cats. "I'm sending this to mum. She won't believe it!"

Grabbing the TV remote, Katherine took a seat at the table. "Not liking the idea of communicating with the kitchen spirit," Katherine said. "How about I turn on the news while you fix some tea? There's honey vanilla in the canister by the stove."

Katherine punched the On button. The TV blared, "Breaking news from Brook County. Sheriff's deputies have found what appears to be the fifth victim in the so-called Festival Murders. The body of a young woman was found dead at the side of a road outside the Erie town limits. The victim's name has not been released, pending notification of relatives. We hope to have an update on the evening news at eleven."

Katherine pushed the Off button. "This is awful," she said. "I feel so terrible for these poor women, and their families and friends."

"What kind of a monster would do such a thing?" Colleen asked, putting the kettle on the stove top.

"Jake said it's rare for serial murders to take place here. I'm terrified to go out at night."

"Well, Katz, then I *wouldn't* go out at night unless you have to."

Iris came into the room and yowled softly. Scout and Abra followed. Abra hopped up onto Katherine's lap and began kneading her arm.

"What's she doing?" Colleen asked with a puzzled expression.

"She's making biscuits."

"Ahhh," Colleen said in wonder. She was still a novice about cat behavior. Changing the subject, she said, "Katz, I can't figure out your new stove. I keep turning the dial and all it does is make a clicking sound. Can you turn it on and watch the kettle. I'm going upstairs to change into my 'ugly' shoes. I'm sure to meet a handsome fireman with the 'ugly' shoes on!"

Katherine set Abra down and said, "Jake should be here in about five minutes."

The doorbell clanged at the carport side of the house. "How about one second," Katherine chuckled rushing to the door. When she opened it, she was surprised to see Jake standing with his cousin Daryl. "Well, hello," she said to Daryl with a smile. "Come in, you two."

Jake said, "Daryl actually got tonight and tomorrow night off, so —"

"I'll be able to come to the party," Daryl finished. "I've been working around the clock with these awful murders. I was surprised the boss let me off. But the State Police is lending a hand. They've formed a special task force."

"Come to the kitchen," Katherine directed. "Colleen is upstairs changing her shoes."

Daryl was staring in awe at the dining room furnishings and wall coverings. "It's like a palace in here," he admired. "I had no idea."

Katherine said, "It looks even grander without the black crepe paper."

Colleen walked into the room. "Oh, I didn't hear anyone come in." She broke into a wide, open smile.

"Colleen, I want to introduce you to Jake Cokenberger."

Jake extended his hand. Shaking it, Colleen said, "Katz has told me so many wonderful things about you."

Jake smiled and winked at Katherine.

"And, this is Jake's cousin Daryl," Katherine said. "Daryl is a deputy for the Brook County Sheriff's Department."

Daryl was speechless for a moment, then said, "I'm pleased to meet you."

"'Tis my pleasure," Colleen said with a slight brogue.

Daryl asked, "Did I hear an Irish accent?"

Colleen threw her head back and said tartly, "No, I'm German."

Daryl belted out the famous Cokenberger laugh, "We're going to get along just fine."

Jake said, "Okay, everybody ready? Let's head to the big fry!"

Katherine looked at her watch and said, "But, it's only six o'clock. I thought we'd hang out a bit. Colleen is making some tea."

"Got to git there before them fish is gone," he said in an exaggerated Hoosier twang.

"Seriously?" Katherine asked.

"Yep. If we go later, there'll be a line like you'll not believe," he explained.

"I'll grab my bag," Katherine said.

"Likewise," Colleen called as she left the room.

Jake said, "We'll head out and meet you fine ladies in front of the house." He wore an amused grin on his face. When they left, Katherine shut and locked the side door.

Colleen came in with her cross-body bag wrapped around her shoulder. She sang a lyric from an Irish folk song, "He whistled and sang 'til the

green woods rang, and he won the heart of a lady."
Katherine joined in the chorus.

Colleen laughed, "Don't give up your day job,
Katz. You still can't sing."

Katherine faked a sad face, and then burst out
laughing. "What's with that German remark? The
poor guy's jaw dropped when he saw you. He could
hardly speak."

"Oh, it was a bit cheeky, but I liked the way he
got my sense of humor. But Katz, why didn't you
warn me that Daryl is a gorgeous hunk?"

Katherine grinned. "Well, it's the Cokenberger
genetics."

"Shut the door! Cokey isn't that hot."

Katherine grinned. "Perhaps he inherited the
recessive genes." Heading to the office, she said,
"My bag's on the desk. I'd better log off the
computer."

Colleen followed and squinted at the web page on the monitor. "Why did you do a search on Mr. Clean?" she asked.

Katherine gave a curious look. "I didn't. It must have been one of the cats." Iris came from behind the monitor and yowled innocently. Katherine picked her up and held her. "Miss Siam, I didn't know *you* surfed the web. Are you trying to tell me something? Maybe something to do with your litterbox?"

"I think we should set up a camera. We could catch who's doing it and put it on YouTube. We can send it to Animal Planet," Colleen said excitedly.

"I believe we've had this conversation before. No way," Katherine countered. "I've already got the looky-loos walking by the pink murder house. I'd really have a problem if they knew my cats surfed the web." Logging off, Katherine observed, "You know in a strange way, one of my students looks like

148

Mr. Clean. My friend Michelle invited him as her guest to the party."

"That's funny. Have the cats ever seen him?"

"During my first lesson, Abra and Scout came into the classroom and saw him then. I guess maybe while we were in the kitchen, Scout or Abra did some cat surfing. Probably Scout. I wouldn't think Abra would have learned that trick so soon. She's only been here a few months."

"'Tis a mystery! Shouldn't we hurry up? The guys are waiting for us."

"I'm done," Katherine announced, getting up from her chair. "Last one to the front door pays the bill."

"Who says? That's ridiculous!" Colleen said, darting in front of Katherine.

"Not fair! I've got to shut the door."

Colleen ran down the front steps and joined Jake and Daryl on the sidewalk.

Katherine locked the front door. "Cheater," she called jokingly to Colleen.

Cokey, Margie, and the two kids pulled up in Cokey's new Dodge Ram crew cab. He yelled out the window, "Hey, are you guys going to the fish fry?"

Jake yelled back, "Yep. Save us a spot at the table!"

"Will do," Cokey said driving away.

Katherine asked, "Which car are we going to take? Obviously, not the Jeep."

Daryl piped in, "My Mercedes is parked in front of the yellow brick house."

All eyes turned in that direction. Colleen said enthusiastically, rushing to the vehicle, "For the love of Mary, you own a '67 Chevy Impala!"

Daryl said, "I'm impressed. How did you know it's an Impala?"

"I watch *Supernatural*. I can see Sam and Dean Winchester spill out of it any moment. It's even black!"

Katherine had never seen her friend so animated. She knew Colleen frequented classic car shows with her four brothers, but she'd never joined them.

Daryl beamed with pride and admiration for Colleen.

Jake offered, "Daryl had it painted. It was originally white."

Colleen gushed, "A four-door sedan. I love it!"

Daryl opened the passenger door for Colleen and she got in. While he was walking over to the driver's side, Jake opened Katherine's door. She slid over so he could sit next to her.

After arriving at the fire station, Daryl was particular about where he parked the classic car. Finally, he decided on a spot two short blocks away. "Got to protect my baby," he apologized.

Colleen said, "Can't blame you."

The four got out and walked to the fish fry. They passed a historic church that was built in the 1840s. They admired the stained glass windows.

"Can we do a selfie in front of it?" Colleen asked. "I want to send it to my mum."

"Sure," Katherine said, leaning into Jake while Colleen did the same with Daryl.

"Perfect," Colleen said, taking the picture. She took a few more pictures, then put her smartphone away.

The Erie fire station was a large, corrugated-metal building of a pole barn design. The fire department comprised both full-time employees and volunteers, who received pay only when actively taking care of an emergency. The volunteers were summoned to duty by a town-wide siren that sounded different from the tornado siren. The fire trucks had been backed out and lined both sides of Main Street. The annual fish fry was the *grand finale* of the Covered Bridge Festival, and residents of the town came out in droves.

The fish fry serving line was beginning to curl around the side of the building.

"I see what you mean," Colleen said.

Daryl gently took her arm and said, "Let's run for it." And, much to Katherine's amazement, Colleen did just that. Katherine thought, *Good thing I suggested the running shoes. She wouldn't have been able to do that with the stilettos.*

"Well," Jake said. "Want to join them?"

Katherine smirked. "Not thinking so. I'll walk. They can save us a place in line."

The line moved quickly. Once inside, Katherine observed rows and rows of long tables set up, covered with decorative orange plastic tablecloths. Each table had a loaf of bread and a tub of butter in the center. Volunteers dished out the food. Katherine's eyes grew big when a woman in her forties handed her a Styrofoam plate with two giant fried fish patties, a large scoop of creamy coleslaw, and a similar size scoop of baked beans. A second table held the drinks and numerous slices of pie and cake in different varieties. When it came to selecting a dessert, she had a hard time narrowing her choices.

Jake helped, "Don't see any coconut cream pie, but German chocolate has coconut. Hey, Colleen, you'll like this. It's German cake."

Colleen laughed and said, "Hilarious!"

Cokey's son, Tommy, ran over to the group while they were paying. "We've saved ya a spot."

Holding large orange trays, Katherine and Jake followed him to the table.

"I want to sit by Jake," Tommy's sister Shelly insisted.

Jake winked and said, "Okay, sweet pea, but Katz sits on my other side. I want to be in the middle of my two favorite girls."

Shelly giggled.

Colleen and Daryl came and sat down.

Cokey said, "Hi, Colleen! I believe the last time I saw you it was in the dead of winter."

Katherine thought, *I hope he doesn't bring up the awful events of that day when his lover killed my boyfriend.*

Instead Cokey said, "I want you to meet my wife, Margie."

"Glad to meet ya," Margie said, leaning over Cokey to shake Colleen's hand. "Katz talks about ya all the time."

Colleen said, "I hope it's the condensed version."

Margie smiled.

They had barely sat down when a fireman came over armed with a large platter of fried fish. "Can I top you off?" he asked the group.

"Not yet," Cokey said, "but keep em' comin'."

Tommy scooted next to his father and said, "Gee, Dad, are you starving or something?"

Shelly snorted like a pig. And, launched into another fit of giggles.

The group was halfway through their meal, when Mark Dunn spotted them, came over, and stood behind Katherine. He leaned over and whispered in her ear, "I approved the Sanders boys hauling away the scrap metal. I told Stevie to call Cokey to schedule a time."

"Why Cokey?" Katherine asked.

"I want Cokey to be there when they show up. Listen, I know I RSVP'd for the party, but something has come up and I can't attend. Will you forgive me?" he asked.

Katherine was surprised. "No problem. We'll miss you, though."

Mark moved over to Colleen's side of the table. "Hello. Katz told me you were coming. How are you?"

Colleen smiled, "I'm just fine, Mark. How are you?"

"Still doing the lawyer thing," he said. "How long are you staying?"

"I leave on Monday."

"What time? I have to drive to Indy for some errands and a noontime seminar. Maybe I can take you to the airport."

"'Twould be grand. My flight leaves in the morning. I think ten o'clock."

"Perfect! I'll pick you up at seven. That will give us plenty of time."

"Super, Mark," Colleen said thankfully.

"We can catch up," he said, eyeing Daryl curiously. He said his goodbyes and left.

Katherine caught Jake and Daryl look at each other questioningly. She wondered if they thought Mark and Colleen had a thing for each other. Then she followed Mark with her eyes. She was curious about whom he was with, but he vanished into the crowd. Once she thought there might be something between them, but after meeting Jake, she knew that wasn't going to happen.

Jake sensed her mood and put his arm around her. "What do you think of the fish fry?" he asked happily.

Before Katherine had time to answer, Barbie Sanders walked by, carrying her tray up high and very close to Katherine's head. She was dressed in a long-sleeved, leopard-printed jumpsuit and matching spiked heels. She pretended to trip, but caught herself.

"Oh, ha! Ha! I'm sorry, Teach. Clumsy of me."

"Hello, Barbie," Katherine said with a nonchalant smile. She didn't want any altercations at the fish fry. Jake turned defensively in his chair. Katherine could tell by his body language that if Barbie messed with her, Jake would intervene.

"Hiss," Barbie spat. "Meow!" she called as she headed for a table filled with other Sanders clan members, who saw the incident and laughed rowdily.

Colleen pointed to her head and mouthed the word, "Nuts!"

Shelly started imitating Barbie. "Meow! Meow! Mom, why did that woman just meow like a cat?"

"Shhh, Shelly," Margie said. "One time she saw Katz's cats in the window."

"Maybe she thinks I'm a crazy cat lady," Katherine joked, trying to reduce the tension at the table. "Okay," she said merrily. "Where's that fireman with the fish?"

Chapter Six

The front doorbell bonged the *Addams Family* famous ringtone with Lurch asking "You rang?" Katherine had it installed just for the party. For fun, she thought about leaving it until Thanksgiving. She darted to open the door.

"You rang?" Mary, the party planner howled with laughter. "Brilliant!"

Mary stood outside with Bella the Russian fortune teller. Misha and the motorhome hadn't arrived yet. Bella was dressed in a colorful purple and black striped gypsy skirt, with a black, long-sleeved peasant blouse. A purple satin sash was tied around her waist. She wore a green turban on her head with a large topaz-colored medallion in front. Her large, gold hoop earrings gleamed in the chandelier's light. Katherine thought with a smile, *She certainly looks the part.*

"Come on in," Katherine said to the two women. "Bella, I believe you wanted to set up in the parlor?"

"Yes," Mary answered for Bella. "Hey, Katz, listen, Misha is running late but he'll definitely be here before the cocktail hour starts."

"That's good to know," Katherine said. "Because his gig takes place *during* the cocktail hour."

Before stepping into the parlor, Mary admired, "I love these black lace panels with the spooky, haunted tree. How clever of you to hang them between the spandrel arches."

"Thanks," Katherine grinned. "I found them online. I like the orange twinkling lights, and my cats like the black Halloween cat and the bat. Oops, better not mention the bat."

Bella flashed a gold-toothed grin and parted the panels. Walking into the parlor, she began moving an Eastlake marble-top table to the center of the room. Mary ran in to help her. Realizing the fortune teller needed a chair, Katherine slid over a velvet-covered Eastlake side chair.

"I think this will work," she said.

"Da," Bella said. "*Spasiba*."

Mary said, "That means 'thank you' in Russian. I've picked up quite a few words."

Bella sat down. Setting her large gypsy bag on the floor next to her, she reached in and withdrew a purple, velvet-fringed tablecloth. She draped it over the table top. Then she reached in her bag and removed a large crystal ball. She set that on the table. She said to Katherine, "Katsee, we do you fortune first."

"Oh, that's not necessary, really," Katherine said, not wanting her fortune told.

Mary insisted, "Oh, Katz, it will be fun. Besides we've got time before the guests arrive. It won't take but a minute."

"I guess," Katherine said reluctantly. She moved a nearby Eastlake side chair in front of the table and sat down.

Bella took Katherine's right hand and turned it over. She began rubbing the lines on Katherine's palm.

"I thought we were doing the crystal ball?" Katherine asked.

Bella brought her finger to her lips. "No speak, Katsee."

"Oh, but that tickles," Katherine giggled. Iris peeked around the corner and quietly watched the group.

"I see much tragedy in your family."

Katherine became very serious and sighed. She thought, *Great! This con artist has heard about the pink murder house.*

Bella continued. "Death haz visited. Much unhappinezz, but three men love you."

Katherine couldn't remain quiet any longer, "Seriously, three? Can you tell me who they are?"

Bella answered, "We move to ze krystal ball." She stared at it intently for a few moments, then said, "Some joy, much sadnezz, and death no ready to leave. More to come."

Mary, who hovered nearby, gasped, "Katz, we don't have to finish this."

"No, I already know I'm Miss Doom-and-Gloom. Please, Bella, do go on."

"Someone you love vill go away. You vill look . . . but no find."

"Can you see who it is?" Katherine asked, worried.

"*Nyet*! Lost." Bella gazed more intently at the ball and said, "Three men. One gone. Two here. One fair; one dark. Does zis mean somezink?"

Katherine put on her best poker face. *She was thinking. Mark Dunn is fair-haired. Jake has dark hair.* She answered, "Not thinking so, but I find this all very interesting. Now if you'll excuse me, I've got a party to put on." Katherine left her chair so abruptly that it rocked back and forth. Iris shot out in front of her, nearly tripping her in the hallway to the back office.

"Look out, Miss Siam. Are you trying to kill the hostess?"

Iris yowled loudly and reached up to be held.

"Okay, Miss Siam," Katherine said, picking her up. She held her and gave her chin scratches. "It's time you go upstairs and join the other cats. We don't want you to get out when the guests arrive. Okay, precious girl?"

"Yowl," Iris replied, lightly biting Katherine's earlobe.

"Well, okay then."

Katherine carried Iris upstairs to her back bedroom. Lilac and Abby were asleep in their cat cozy cube on the ornate renaissance-revival bed, while Scout and Abra were sitting on the windowsill looking out. Katherine set Iris on the floor and then left. Closing the door, she turned the key in the deadbolt lock and went back downstairs to join Colleen in the kitchen. She found Colleen helping Vicky, the Erie Hotel caterer, arrange hors d'oeuvres on a platter.

"Katz, try this," Colleen said, handing Katherine an appetizer with layers of thinly sliced mozzarella cheese, basil leaf, and tomato, arranged on a Breton cracker.

"Oh, my God," Katherine sighed with closed eyes. "This reminds me of our favorite wine and cheese place on 53rd Street."

"Uh-huh," Colleen agreed. "I forgot to compliment you earlier. I like the way you decorated the dining room," she admired.

Katherine smiled. "The ceiling height is so tall, I asked Cokey to set up a tall ladder so I could hot glue the black crepe paper to the upper plate rail, then run it over and attach it to the cranberry glass chandelier."

"The plastic bat is pretty cool too. I like the way it hangs from the crystal chandelier. Where did you find a black tablecloth and those sweet dishes?"

"An online Halloween party store. Colleen, I need you to help me with something."

"Sure."

"See those gothic-looking place cards? I need to figure out who's sitting next to whom, and arrange the place cards around the table."

"Well, first of all, you'll be sitting next to Jake. I want to be sitting next to Daryl. So everyone else can grab their card and sit wherever they want," Colleen said mischievously.

Katherine laughed, "You're a big help! Jake suggested we do boy-girl, boy-girl. So, at the head of the table closest to the carport door I'll put Jake. On Jake's right, I'll sit, which is closest to the kitchen door, in case Carson the Butler isn't available."

Colleen said in her best Downton Abbey Lady Mary accent, "I really think the Colfax Abbey needs another footman to serve, preferably one who looks like Tom Branson."

"Of course, you'd say Tom Branson! Would his being Irish have anything to do with it?"

"Just sayin.' Tom and Daryl do sort of look-alike in a blond, green-eyed sort of way," Colleen said with an impish grin.

Katherine giggled. "Margie will sit next to you on the right. Cokey will be at the other end of the table. Michelle will sit to Cokey's right. Then her date, Glen, will sit on her right. Leslie and Jake's friend, Wayne, will sit to the left of Jake."

"What a science! Yes, boy-girl, boy-girl. I know that Mark Dunn isn't coming, but who was the twelfth person who couldn't come?" Colleen asked.

"Detective Linda Martin. I so wanted her to come. Since the speakeasy find, I've had lunch with her several times. She's really cool. Plus she loves cats!"

"I remember her from last winter. Why can't she come?"

"She's lead detective on the Festival Murders case. She told me she's working long hours interviewing lots of people."

A middle-aged man with a crop of gray hair walked in and announced, "I'm the bartender."

"Frank." Katherine recognized him. "I thought you worked at the diner?"

"Yeppers, but I bartend on the weekends for the Erie Hotel. Where do you want me to set up the bar?" he asked, struggling with a large carton of wine, beer, and liquor bottles.

"Follow me," Katherine said, walking into the decorated living room. The Victorian furniture had been pushed back against the walls, so there was room in the middle for guests to mingle. The fireplace mantel held six pottery pumpkins with tea lights inside. A large, black flowered wreath was placed on a hook above the mirror. Katherine pointed to a sideboard with a mottled pink marble-top. "How about there?"

"Looks mighty fancy to me," Frank said with an admiring glance.

"Kindly suggestion. If you spill anything, could you quickly wipe it up? The marble is more forgiving than the wood. I've learned that the hard way," Katherine said.

"Yeppers, nothin' like leavin' a big ugly ring when you set a drink down."

"Thanks, really appreciate it," Katherine said, leaving. She headed back to the kitchen to talk to Colleen. Colleen was busy sampling another appetizer.

"Busted," Colleen said, with a miniature puffed pastry in her mouth. "These are to die for."

The caterer smiled and handed Katherine one. "Vicky, these look wonderful," Katherine said, as she bit into it. The pastry exploded with cheese and broccoli cascading down her blouse.

Colleen smirked, "Just like old times. Got any seltzer?"

Katherine grabbed a washrag and dabbed at the stain. "Oh, that will have to do." She then grabbed Colleen's arm. "Okay, it's your turn to see the fortune teller."

Colleen protested mildly. "I guess, but you know that woman is a fraud, right? She's a cold reader. She asks you a question, then reads your body language for the answer."

"Oh, forget that. Just have fun with it. I'll wait outside."

"No, I insist you stay in the room with me!" Colleen demanded.

Katherine and Colleen headed for the dining room, but caught Jake in the atrium. Jake wore a huge grin.

Katherine observed, "You look like the cat that swallowed the canary. What gives?"

Jake shrugged, "Nothing. Madame Bella just gave me the best news."

"Really?" Katherine said incredulously, not thinking Jake would be one to have his fortune told. Jake grabbed her and kissed her cheek. The doorbell sounded, "You rang?" "I'll get it," he said, moving away.

"I wonder what she told him," Colleen kidded.

"Madame Bella," Katherine let out a laugh. "Jake's always naming things."

When Colleen and Katherine walked into the parlor, Bella was peering into a hand mirror, adjusting the turban on her head. When she saw the two friends, she quickly put the mirror in her bag.

"Your turn, Colleen. I was her first victim."

Colleen sat down on the Eastlake side chair. Bella began reading Colleen's palm. Colleen was too busy looking out the large picture window at Daryl, who had just parked and was getting out of his car. She wasn't paying attention to Bella's predictions until Bella announced, "You make big move – many miles – to join your loved one."

Startled, Colleen snapped out of her Daryl-induced trance. "Seriously?" she asked, flipping her hair back defiantly. "Joining Mario? *That* will be the day!" She got up abruptly, and almost tripped over the threshold rushing to the door to greet Daryl.

In the meantime, Wayne Watson and Leslie had arrived and were talking to Jake. Katherine walked over to guide them to the living room.

"I'm so glad you came. Can I get you a drink?" Katherine asked, playing the part of a perfect hostess.

Leslie said in her quiet voice, "I'll have a gin and tonic." Wayne said, "I'm driving, so I'll have a Coke."

Katherine nodded toward Frank. "Well guys, that gentleman standing over there will fix you right up." She led them over to the bar.

Frank said, "I heard it! One gin and tonic, one Coke, coming your way. Ms. Kendall, what do you want?"

"I'm good," she said, then to Wayne, "How did you two meet? Do you both share the metal detecting hobby?"

Leslie answered, "We met last July in San Diego at Comic Con."

"Yeah," Wayne said, "We were surprised we're both from the same city."

"That's so cool," Katherine said, leaving them to rejoin Jake at the front door.

When Daryl came in, he said hello to Jake and Katherine, then when he saw Colleen, his face lit up like a Christmas tree.

"Hi, Colleen," he said cheerfully. Colleen took him by the arm and said, "I've got to show you something that's really cool!" She then led him upstairs. When Daryl turned on the first stairwell landing, he gave Jake a look of curious wonderment.

Jake winked. Katherine nudged him in the ribs. Then Cokey and Margie entered, holding hands.

"Look at you two," Katherine teased.

Margie said, "Yep, kiddo, tonight is date night. The kids are at grandpa and grandma Cokenberger's, being spoiled rotten." Margie hugged Katherine,

"Gee, you've really decorated up the place. Good show!" she complimented. "All this really goes with the gargoyles out front."

"Come in the living room," Jake directed.

Cokey asked Jake, "Where's the cats?"

"Oh, Katz locked them upstairs. With people coming in and out, she didn't want them to get out."

The doorbell sounded "You rang?" Katherine hurried to open it. It was her two students, Michelle and Glen, on their first date.

Michelle said, "I think the library needs an Addams Family doorbell. Kids would love it."

Glen reached over and hugged Katherine and kissed her cheek. Katherine thought it was a little too friendly, and was speechless for a moment. She finally said, "Please come into the living room. We've got the bar set up there."

As they walked in, Katherine observed a pretty young girl with dark hair pulled back in a ponytail; she was passing out appetizers. Glen made a beeline for her and said, "Hey, Tiffany, I didn't know you were working here tonight." He gave the young woman a big hug, and she nearly dropped the tray. He then used the most cheesy chat-up line of the century: "If I told you that you had a nice body, would you hold it against me?" The young woman's face turned beet-red, and she moved away. But Glen followed her, totally ignoring his date.

Colleen and Daryl walked in. Colleen was smiling. Daryl joined Jake and Cokey, who were loading up on the puffy cheese pastries. Katherine advised, "Beware! They explode at will." She pointed at the wet stain on her blouse.

Katherine whispered to Colleen, "What gives? What did you have to show Daryl?"

"My spirit hunting equipment. Last night at the fish fry, he said he was interested. Later, we're going to explore the attic."

"But what about the bats up there?" Katherine reminded.

"I'll let Daryl handle that part of it," Colleen smirked.

"Just make sure when you conjure up a ghost, you tell it to leave when you're finished with it. Oh, and keep the attic door closed," Katherine advised.

Katherine stepped over to the front turret window and looked for Misha's motorhome. He still hadn't arrived. He was very late. Since he was the entertainment for the cocktail hour, Katherine searched for the party planner and found her in the kitchen. She was exchanging recipes with Vicky.

"Mary," Katherine interrupted. "Where's Misha?"

"Oh, I just talked to him. He's almost here."

"Great! Could you meet him at the door and tell him to come to the living room and start his gig?" Katherine directed. "You did remind him we weren't doing the pickpocket part until I'd okayed it with the guests?"

"Oh, yes," Mary assured her.

The doorbell rang. Katherine started to answer it, but couldn't resist another puffy cheese pastry, which once again exploded on the front of her blouse. "Dammit!" she said.

"Take this," Vicky said, handing a damp rag to Katherine. "It's got your name on it," she said in jest.

"No, I'm going to take the back stairs and go up to my room and change. The entire front of my blouse is wet." Katherine opened the kitchen stairwell door and ran up the rickety steps. She walked to her great aunt's old bedroom, which she had converted into a dressing room. She changed into another blouse and then walked back down to join the party. By the time she got to the living room, Misha had arrived and all hell had broken loose.

Daryl had Misha in a chokehold. When Misha saw Katherine, he gasped in a hoarse voice, "Katsee . . . help?"

"Oh, my gawd!" Katherine yelled. "Daryl, please let him go."

Daryl protested. "He stole my wallet!"

Katherine tried to explain. "It's part of his close-up magic. I'm so sorry."

Daryl released his grasp. Misha brushed the front of his purple velvet jacket more out of embarrassment than if any bodily harm had been done.

Katherine began to explain, "Misha didn't read the memo about not doing this act until I'd talked to you all about it. We're going to have a scavenger's hunt. The person who finds the most items will win a gift card worth fifty bucks."

"Yay," Michelle said. Glen was at her side, but he was still eyeing Tiffany.

Katherine said to Misha, "Did you pickpocket anyone else?"

Misha wore a guilty expression and put his hands in his roomy pockets. Extracting stolen objects with both hands, he placed them in a large Imari bowl nearby on the marble-top coffee table. He drew out a rabbit's foot, a gold bracelet, a USB thumb drive, a hair clippy, a set of keys, a calculator, a Claddagh ring, a diamond ring, and Lilac's bear.

The guests began talking a mile a minute.

"Hey, give me Hewie back," Wayne demanded, as he pointed at his calculator. Leslie piped in, "That's my hair thingy."

Cokey said, "That's my rabbit's foot!" Margie added, "I'll need those keys!"

"The thumb drive is mine," Michelle said, giggling. "How did you do it? It's amazing. I didn't feel a thing."

Katherine said, "I had Lilac's bear in my pocket. Misha, she'll want it back."

"That's my Claddagh ring," Colleen accused. "My Aunt Eileen gave it to me."

Jake moved over to the Imari bowl. "The diamond ring is mine." He fished the ring out and swiftly put it in his pocket.

Katherine gave Jake a curious look, but he only smiled. Glen started to step forward but Katherine darted ahead of him. She snatched the bear out of the bowl and put it back in her pocket. Then, she announced to the group, "These were the items to be hidden in the scavenger hunt. My party planner was going to create a map of where the items would be hidden in the house. After dinner we were going to search for them, but – "

Cokey interrupted, "Sounds like fun, as long as we get our stuff back."

"Definitely," Katherine assured him, as she wondered why on earth she'd thought the scavenger hunt would be a fun idea.

Margie clapped her hands. "I want to win the gift card!"

Daryl said in a firm voice to Misha, "My wallet isn't part of the game. Hand it over."

Misha slowly handed it to the deputy. Daryl searched its contents to make sure everything was there.

Tiffany walked in carrying another tray of appetizers. The group gathered around her. Michelle moved to Frank's station for another cocktail, while Glen hung around Tiffany.

Katherine picked up the Imari bowl and headed to the back office. Misha followed her and apologized, "Katsee, so sorry. Got confoosed."

"No problem," Katherine answered, but wondered if he'd been confused or not. Maybe he'd been ripping off guests and Mary didn't know anything about it.

Mary was at the keyboard typing instructions; she was completely oblivious as to what had just transpired. She asked Misha, "How many items did you snatch?" Then noticing Katherine, "Oh, hi, Katz."

Katherine handed her the Imari bowl with the stolen items in it.

"Seven stay," Misha said in his thick Russian accent.

"Okay, I'll make up seven envelopes."

Katherine said, "I'll leave you two to do your thing. Oh, and Misha, word of advice, don't go near Daryl again."

"Da, Katsee," Misha said rubbing the back of his neck.

Katherine went into the kitchen. Vicky said, "We just unloaded the van. Dinner can be served at any moment."

"Was that the last of the appetizers?"

"Yes."

"Okay, we'll probably sit down to dinner in ten minutes. Thanks." Katherine started to leave and then walked back. "Vicky, not that I'm being nosy or anything, but Glen seems to be paying loads of attention to Tiffany. He's Michelle's date, but he can't take his eyes off Tiffany."

Vicky put her hand on her hip and said matter-of-factly, "Glen hits on *all* the gals who work at the Hotel. Tiffany's engaged to a student at the university. She'll be helping me in the kitchen, if that's okay with you."

"Oh, that's fine," Katherine said evasively. She didn't want the rest of the evening spoiled for Michelle by her flirtatious date-from-hell.

"Frank will take Tiffany's place and serve. By the way, do you know who Tiffany's uncle is?"

"No, who?" Katherine asked.

"She's Chief London's niece. His brother's daughter."

"That's good to know," Katherine said. "I really appreciate your helping out tonight."

"We aim to please," Vicky said. "Oh, a question. Is it all right if we leave through the basement? I thought after we'd cleared the table and washed the dishes, the three of us would leave. Frank's doing the eleven-to-seven shift at the diner. Don't know what Tiffany's doing, but I'm all tuckered out."

"Sure, that's fine."

*   *   *

As the guests left the party, each expressed thanks and said how much fun they had. Jake stood next to Katherine at the front door. The scavenger hunt had been a huge success, but no matter how much the guests searched the pink mansion, following Mary's precise map, they couldn't find the last item. Katherine tried to call the party planner for more information, but she wasn't picking up, so she left a voice mail. She'd look for the seventh envelope later and return it to its rightful owner tomorrow. The guests counted the items they'd found. Michelle discovered the most and was the happy winner. She quickly pocketed her fifty dollar gift card. Then the guests exchanged items until each had his or her own. Cokey thought it was a hoot that his old rabbit's foot was lifted by the magician, but Margie wasn't amused. She said she was concerned because the key belonged to the yellow brick house next door. But it all turned out as just old-fashioned fun. While Michelle headed for the door, Daryl and Colleen were exchanging email addresses. Katherine said to Michelle, "Sorry about Glen having to run out."

"Me, too," Michelle said. "Some date. He got sick right after dinner. Hope he's going to be okay. He promised to call me tomorrow," then she whispered, "I hope he doesn't. Did you see the way he was hitting on Tiffany?"

"Sorry to say," Katherine sympathized. "See you Monday."

Michelle walked to the door. "Thanks for inviting me. I had a fun time," she said as she left.

Daryl came over and hugged Katherine. He said, "It was fun. I had a great time." Then he whispered in Katherine's ear, "Jake is lucky to have found you." He then smiled a big Cokenberger grin and left. He called back to Jake, "See you tomorrow."

"Sure thing," Jake said, then to Katherine, "Daryl is coming out to my place to help with the leaves. It's a mess out there. If you're not doing anything, why don't you bring Colleen. I bet she's never seen a Hoosier windmill."

"Sounds like a great idea."

Wayne and Leslie walked out together, saying that they had a fun time. "I nearly had a heart attack when that magician stole Hewie," Wayne said, patting his front T-shirt pocket. "Hey, next time you have a scavenger hunt, let me know in advance so I can bring my detector." Leslie poked him in the arm and they left, heading for Wayne's car.

Colleen excused herself and said she was heading upstairs. She said to Jake, "I couldn't help but overhear, and I can help rake leaves."

"Cool, then it's a done deal," Jake said with a smile.

Colleen walked upstairs singing the Irish folksong. "And, he won the heart of a lady . . . ."

Jake took Katherine in his arms and kissed her tenderly. "The party was a huge success. I give it five stars. I think everyone had a great time. I'll see you tomorrow," he said, opening the door and leaving.

Chapter Seven

Katherine stood at the door and fondly watched Jake get in his Jeep and drive away. She had just engaged the thumb turn on the deadbolt when Colleen flew down the stairs.

"Katz, there's something wrong with the cats. They're making all sorts of noise."

"What's going on? I can hear them," Katherine tensely answered. She lunged up the stairs with Colleen close behind.

Standing outside the bedroom door, Katherine and Colleen could hear the cats shrieking inside; the caterwauling was deafening. Katherine hurriedly turned the key and opened the door. Scout and Abra shot out and thundered down the hall. Abby was on top of the headboard pediment, cowering. Her tail was three times its normal size. "Chirp," she peeped in a frightened tone.

"What the hell?" Katherine said, then gasped. "Oh, my God! The window's open." Katherine rushed over and closed it.

"Oh, for the love of Mary," Colleen said, shocked.

"We've got to find Iris and Lilac." Katherine fell to her knees and peered under the renaissance-revival bed. "Colleen, hand me that flashlight hanging on the door."

Colleen found the light and turned it on. Handing it to Katherine, she said, "They're probably in the bed lining like that time at the hotel in Pennsylvania."

"Come here, babies," Katherine said in a calming voice. "Where are you, my darlings?"

Lilac flew out from under the bed and leaped into Katherine's arms. "Me-yowl," she cried nervously.

Katherine held her close. "It's okay, sweet girl. Calm down. It's okay. Where's Iris?"

Lilac continued me-yowling in a shrill Siamese voice. When Abby jumped down from the headboard, Colleen quickly picked her up.

"Let's move them to the front of the hall and put them in my great aunt's old bedroom," Katherine said. "When we catch Scout and Abra, we'll put them in there too."

"But where's Iris?" Colleen asked worriedly, holding Abby securely while following Katherine down the hall.

"I'm praying she's in the bed lining. The worst case scenario, she dove out the bedroom window. She could be out there right now on the damned carport roof."

Katherine opened the front bedroom door and gently put Lilac down. Colleen set Abby down next to her. Shutting the door, Katherine raced back to her bedroom, calling Iris's name in a soft tone.

Colleen rushed after her and said, "Katz, I don't want to freak you out, but why would the window be open? It's on the second story."

Katherine didn't answer, but opened the window again and shone the flashlight around the perimeter. "I'm going to climb out there."

"What? No way!" Colleen said uneasily.

"Grab that small step ladder behind the door."

Colleen found the ladder and handed it to Katherine. Katherine took the ladder, passed it through the window opening, and opened its legs. She placed it on the metal roof of the carport. She then heaved herself through the window opening, one leg at a time, and stepped down to the flat roof.

Colleen worried. "But isn't it dangerous? What if you fall?"

"Not likely. This once was a sleeping porch," Katherine explained. "Years ago someone replaced the door with a window. Now it's just the carport roof." Katherine beamed the flashlight along the wood balusters. "Colleen, Margie's been painting these, so I unlocked the window so she could climb in to use the bathroom." She carefully walked to the center of the metal roof.

Colleen leaned out. "Do you think Margie left the window open?"

"It was shut when I put the kids in here, but I don't remember locking it. I guess I was just too wrapped up in the party."

Katherine took one last look outside and then saw a folded envelope immediately underneath the window. "What the hell," she said. Reaching down to pick it up, she was startled to see it was the missing scavenger hunt envelope. The number seven was written in bold on front.

Wondering how the envelope wound up in such a strange place, she thrust it in her pocket. Climbing back into the room, Katherine said, "She's got to be under the bed. I'll check again." She fell to her knees and shone the light back-and-forth underneath, as well as along the perimeter. "Miss Siam, it's okay. You can come out now," she coaxed. "Treat! Treat!" she called, to no avail.

Colleen asked, "Why did you leave so much money on the dresser? There's quite a bit of cash sitting there."

"What do you mean?" Katherine said, getting back up and moving to the dresser.

"Look, it's hundred dollar bills," Colleen said, handing the money to Katherine.

"I didn't put it there," Katherine said apprehensively. "What's this?" she asked, picking up a nearby party invitation. "I didn't put that there, either." Inside someone had drawn a cartoon outline of a Siamese with a smiley face below it. A thousand thoughts flashed through Katherine's mind. She remembered the front porch incident with Barbie and her brother, Bobby, discussing Scout and Abra in the window. She could hear Barbie's voice in the classroom, "How much would they sell for?"

"No-o-o-o," Katherine screamed. "I think that freaking Barbie woman stole Iris."

Colleen opened the invitation and read it. She looked at Katherine skeptically. "Katz, why would you think that from a cat drawing and a smiley face?"

"I know it's her. I've got to call Chief London," Katherine said as a tear slid down her cheek. She yanked out her cell, scrolled down her contacts list, then tapped on the chief's number. It rang and rang and then went into voice mail. "Chief, it's Katz Kendall. Someone broke into my house and stole my cat. Please call me as soon as possible."

Colleen was standing close to the door. She was startled when Scout and Abra came back in, brushing past her.

Scout sprang from the windowsill to the dresser and began licking the glossy photo front of the invitation. "Gimme that," Katherine said, snatching it away from her and tossing it in the top drawer. She picked up her resident drug addict and gently hugged her. "Scout, if only you could talk and tell me who took Iris."

"Ma-waugh," Scout cried at the mention of Iris's name.

Abra jumped and walked across the bed, leaving a trail of bloody paw prints on the white comforter. "Katz, she's got blood on her paws!"

Katherine didn't hesitate. "I've got to check both of them to make sure they're not hurt." Katherine picked up Abra, who trembled and collapsed against her. "Raw," she cried. Katherine hurried to the bathroom and set Abra on the counter. She examined her, but found no cuts or wounds. Then, Katherine spread one of Abra's front paws and noticed that two of her claws were broken to the quick. Katherine called to Colleen, who was still in the bedroom. "Could you come in here and grab something for me?"

"Sure. Where?" Colleen asked, hurrying in.

Still holding Abra, Katherine pointed with her nose. "Top drawer on the left. There's a plastic box with cotton swabs in it. There's a cat on the label."

Colleen opened the drawer and removed the container. "What do I do now?" Colleen asked, grimacing when she saw Abra's broken claws. "Oh, you poor darlin'."

"Take out a swab and flick it. It's got antiseptic in it. I'm going to hunker over Abra and put some of that stuff on her broken claws."

"But Katz, that might hurt like hell," she said with concern.

"I know. I can't help it. I don't want her to get an infection."

Colleen snapped the swab and handed it to Katherine.

Abra was a wonderful patient because she didn't move, flinch or struggle while Katherine applied the antiseptic. "You're such a good girl," Katherine cooed, kissing the Siamese on the head.

"Raw," Abra said sweetly, then escaped Katherine's arms and sprang to the floor. Surprised, Katherine said, "Dammit! I was going to put her in with the other cats." They could hear Abra scamper down the hall. "Scout, your turn." Scout didn't want any part of it and chased after her feline sister.

"This is really gross, Colleen, but I think I saw bits of human skin in-between Abra's claws. I'm banking whoever took Iris suffered some pretty deep scratches."

"Katz, forget about the chief returning your call. Let's just call 9-1-1. We can tell the police your suspicion. Maybe the Erie police can check the local hospital to find out if anyone came in with animal wounds. It's worth a try."

"It had to have been Barbie. And her brother, Bobby, probably helped her," Katherine accused.

"How did they get up here?" Colleen asked.

"That damn scaffolding is still set up. They climbed up to the carport roof, then just opened the window. Now I'm worried about how they carried Iris down." Katherine brought her hand up to stifle a sob.

"Oh, Katz," Colleen said, moving over. She put her arm around her shoulder. "We'll find her."

Katherine cried, "Have you ever climbed scaffolding? It takes two hands. How could she hold a Siamese as feisty as Iris and climb down at the same time? It's impossible!"

Colleen shook her head and said in a low voice, "Katz, maybe that Russian guy stole her. You've gotta remember. He *really* liked her."

Katz looked up, startled. "Remember when I first met him and he kept trying to buy things from me? 'Make a bizz-ness,' he kept saying. I guess he did make a business because he left money on the dresser." Counting it, Katherine said, "It's the three hundred dollars I paid him for his gig."

Colleen got up and grabbed her cell phone. She dialed 9-1-1. The Erie dispatcher picked up immediately.

"9-1-1. What's your emergency?" the woman asked.

"I want to report a burglary or maybe a home invasion. Katherine Kendall's house. Yes, yes. The pink one on Lincoln Street. Okay, we will." Colleen ended the call. "We're supposed to stay put until the police come."

"Okay," Katherine said, fishing out her cell and calling Jake. He answered right away.

"Jake, can you come back? Something terrible has happened. Someone climbed the scaffolding and broke into my bedroom where the cats were. They've taken Iris," Katherine said, her voice breaking. "Colleen just called the police."

"Who the hell would do such a thing? Katz, I'm literally stuck in traffic. I'm just a few miles from the turn off road to my house. There's some sort of police action going on up ahead. Flashing lights everywhere. It's probably another bust at the Sanders trailer court. I'm going to put the Jeep in four-wheel drive and take the shoulder. Maybe that way I can get out of this jam and head back to the mansion. Hang on a minute while I do that." There was a pause, then Jake came back on and said firmly, "Katz, lock the door to the room you're in and stay there until the police get there. Usually, burglaries involve two or more people working together. Someone else might still be in the house."

"I can't," Katherine cried. "Scout and Abra are loose. Lilac and Abby are in another room."

"Then you need to get Colleen and the cats and get the hell out of the house. Go to the bungalow. I'll try my best to get there as soon as possible." He hung up.

"What's going on?" Colleen asked anxiously.

"Jake wants us to get out of the house."

"But what about the police? They're coming."

"Colleen, it's a small town. Jake said there's some kind of police action. He's stuck in traffic.

That means the chief and officers are tied up with that. He wants us to go to the bungalow."

Scout and Abra were outside the door, growling and hissing.

Katherine and Colleen both heard a floorboard creak in the hall. Colleen brought her hand up to block a scream. Katherine lunged for the tall armoire and opened a drawer to her gun safe. She touched the keypad and then yanked out a Glock. Flipping the safety off, she ran into the hall. A man or woman – she couldn't tell which – was turning toward the stairwell. Dressed in black, complete with pulled up hoodie, the figure was chased by Scout and Abra.

"Stop right there," Katherine shouted. "Or I'll shoot you dead!" she threatened.

The intruder ran down the stairs, taking four or five steps at a time. Katherine was close behind, but wasn't fast enough to see who it was, or to catch up.

The trespasser fumbled for the door lock, found it, and ran out the front door. When Katherine got to the foot of the stairs, she could see Abra dash to the back office; her tail was puffed up. Scout flew out the opened front door with Katherine chasing her. The person in the hoodie had vanished into the night.

Katherine was terrified that Scout would run out into the street, but Scout stopped on the sidewalk just in front of where Misha's motorhome had been parked during the party. She began swaying back and forth.

Katherine sprinted toward her. "It's okay, baby. Just stay there," she said softly. She prayed Scout wouldn't bolt into the night, but Scout stayed put, arching her back and hopping up and down like an agitated Halloween cat. A car with high beams was speeding down Lincoln Street. When Scout was momentarily distracted, Katherine tackled the Siamese and snatched her around the middle. With the startled cat in her arms, she returned to the pink mansion.

Colleen was looking out the front sidelight window and quickly opened the door. "Did you see who it was?"

"No, dammit." Scout struggled to get down, but Katherine held her tight. With one hand she held Scout and then locked the door.

"Katz, when you ran downstairs, I darted in my room and grabbed my bag. The window screen was lying on the floor and the window was open."

"You've got to be kidding me. Another window? How many windows are unlocked up there?" Katherine said disgustedly.

"I think that's how they got in," Colleen said. "While we were in your bedroom, they must have climbed up and come through my room's window."

"Colleen, we've got to get out of here. Help me find Abra."

"I saw her run after you."

"I saw her head toward the back of the house, but I wanted to make sure she didn't backwash and run upstairs. I've got two carriers in the office. Let's put Scout in, then find Abra."

Scout began squirming even more. "Stop fighting me," Katherine pleaded.

The two jogged to the back of the house, shutting several doors behind them to thwart Abra's possible escape.

"Katz, are you sure no one else is in the house?" Colleen worried.

"No, at this point, I'm not sure of anything, but I've got my Glock," Katherine reassured.

"You're freaking me out. When did you get a gun?" Colleen asked in disbelief, but Katherine was already in a different room and didn't hear her. She grabbed two cat carriers out of the closet and opened the metal door of the first one. She gently put Scout in.

"Waugh," Scout objected. As if on cue for an important close-up in a movie, Abra trotted around the corner and miraculously shot for the carrier. Katherine barely had time to open the metal door, when Abra leaped in. "Raw," Abra said quietly. She began licking Scout's ears. "Good girls," Katherine praised.

"Now what?" Colleen whispered.

"Here's the plan. We'll carry the cats to the side vestibule. You'll stay with them behind the closed door. I'm going back upstairs to get Lilac and Abby."

"Katz, can't I go with you? I'll be down here without a *Glock*."

"I'm not going to leave you here without a weapon. Just help me do this."

The two reached down, each taking one end of the carrier, and moved the cats through the dining room into a small vestibule leading to the carport exit door.

Katherine spotted Cokey's toolbox in the corner – one he'd forgotten to take home – and lifted up the lid. She pulled out a large claw hammer. She handed it to Colleen, "Okay, if anyone gets in here, hit them with this."

Colleen's eyes were wide with terror. "Are you crazy, Katz? I can't do that!"

"I'm sure you won't have to. Both of the doors between the dining room and the carport are made of solid oak. It would take *Superman* to break them down," Katherine explained. She grabbed a door security bar, handed it to Colleen, and stepped through the doorway. "Prop this on the door. I'll only be a few minutes." Katherine didn't wait for an answer, but shut the door with Colleen and Scout and Abra on the other side.

Katherine dashed upstairs holding the gun in one hand and the second carrier in the other. She opened the bedroom door and found Abby and Lilac cowering in the corner. She placed the Glock in the back of her jeans waistband and said in a soothing voice, "It's going to be okay. Come to mommy." Katherine picked up both of them and gently placed them in the carrier. Lilac didn't start me-yowling loudly until the metal grille door was closed. Then she launched into a barrage of Siamese protests. Abby countered by growling. Katherine slowly ambled to the stairs and struggled to carry the cage down. She returned to the side door and jiggled the knob.

"Colleen, open up. It's me."

Colleen cautiously opened the door.

"Okay, we're good to go," Katherine said. "I don't think there's anyone else in the house, but I don't want to stay and find out."

"Katz, when did you get a gun?" Colleen said, still asking questions about the Glock.

"I've had it since last summer. Don't worry. I know how to use it. I took a handgun safety course. Jake and I joined a gun club. I practice every other weekend." The cats began to caterwaul loudly. "Shhh! It's okay, my treasures. We'll be at the bungalow soon." Then to Colleen, "I'm glad I re-parked right outside the door." Katherine pressed the key fob and the car doors automatically unlocked. "Can you carry a carrier by yourself? I know it's heavy."

"I can. Let's do it," Colleen said, lifting Scout's and Abra's carrier.

"Follow me," Katherine said, picking up Lilac and Abby. "Watch your step. I'll open the back hatch." At the bottom of the side carport steps, Katherine looked up and down the driveway to see if the coast was clear. She was surprised to see Stevie Sanders walking over from the carriage house. She didn't recognize him at first because he had cut his hair.

"What are you doing here?" she asked, frightened.

Stevie saw the two of them holding cat carriers. "Need any help?" he offered.

"No, we're fine," Katherine said warily.

"Look, I'm trying to find Cokey for the key. No one answered at his house," Stevie said.

Katherine mused and said to herself, *It's date night, you idiot*.

She set her carrier in the back of the Subaru while Colleen did the same. With lightning speed, Colleen got into the vehicle.

Katherine shut the hatch, then asked Stevie. "Where are you parked?"

"The guys are parked in the alley behind the carriage house."

Katherine called to Colleen, "I'll be back in a minute."

Colleen mouthed the words, "Hurry up!"

"I've got a key. I'll let you in. Why did you pick tonight to haul away the stuff?"

"Got a construction job out-of-town. This is the only time I can do it. Sellin' the scrap to pay for gas," he said in an apologetic tone.

"Is Barbie with you?" Katherine asked. "I need to ask her something." She thought, *I need to ask her if she stole Iris.*

"Nope, haven't seen her. Why?"

Katherine didn't answer but put the key in the padlock and opened the lock. She turned to Stevie.

"Do me a favor? Take whatever metal my great aunt promised you, but please don't take my rake or garden tools."

Stevie smiled. The overhead carriage house light caught the gold glint on his front tooth. "Hey, thanks. Would you like to have dinner with me some night? I'd carry you out for a steak."

"I'm seeing someone, but thanks for offering." She quickly made her way back to the Subaru, sprang in, fired up the engine and pulled forward. She drove to the service alley behind the carriage house. True to Stevie's word, the two pickup trucks were parked behind with their truck lights on. He waved to her while she turned right.

Pulling out onto U.S. 41, Colleen broke the silence. "He's really good looking for a crim."

"That crim just asked me out for a date."

"Shut the door! He didn't."

217

"Waugh," "Raw," "Me-yowl," the Siamese complained. Abby trilled a loud chirp.

"It's okay my sweet girls," Katherine said in a quiet voice. "Colleen, I should have picked up the money and party invitation to show the chief."

"Katz, before I came downstairs, I took the invitation out of the drawer, along with the money, and put them in my bag."

"Good work! Did you rotate the thumb turn on the door lock?"

"I don't remember," Colleen admitted. "I think I did."

"Maybe I'll be lucky and the Sanders bunch will walk into the house and catch the home invader," Katherine said sarcastically. "I'm not going to worry about it."

"Ma-waugh," Scout scolded.

"So where's the bungalow?" Colleen asked.

"Not far," Katherine said.

Colleen persisted. "Do you still have the key? I mean, are you still renting it?"

"I bought it when I received the six-month distribution from the estate. I went to the bank and took out a mortgage."

"Wow. And you didn't tell me," Colleen said, a little hurt that her best friend had kept something of that magnitude a secret.

"I planned on showing you the house tomorrow, but I guess you'll get to see it tonight."

"If it's not far from the mansion, why haven't we gotten there yet?"

Katherine explained. "I've watched too many scary movies to know the bad guy follows the good guy home, so I'm going to drive around Erie for a bit." She drove to various places of business, pulled in, then turned around and steered to the next. When she was comfortable no one was following her, she drove to the bungalow and parked in the lane by the side of the house. Jake was already there, sitting on the front porch steps. She could see Cokey briskly walking down the sidewalk from his house several doors down.

Katherine and Colleen got out of the car.

Jake ran over to Katherine and embraced her. "Katz, are you okay?"

"Yes, we're good. Can you help me carry the cats?"

Cokey sprinted to them, "Geez, I'm out of shape," he said, slightly out of breath.

Katherine directed Colleen to the front door. She opened the door, but didn't turn on any lights. Cokey and Jake each took hold of a cat carrier and followed Katz and Colleen inside.

"Follow me to the kitchen in the back," Katherine said. The street light outside illuminated the room enough to enable them to move back to the kitchen without tripping over anything. Then she closed the wooden slats of the kitchen window blind and turned on the counter lamp.

Still holding the cat carrier with Lilac and Abby in it, Cokey asked, "Where should I put them?"

Jake answered, "I'll show you. We'll put them in one of the bedrooms." While the two men were out of earshot, Katherine said to Colleen, "This is a nightmare. How could anyone steal one of my kids?"

Cokey and Jake returned.

"Okay, so all hell broke loose after the party," Cokey began. "Jake called me and told me what happened."

Katherine sat down on the bench of the built-in table, while Colleen stood nervously nearby.

Katherine slid over so Jake could join her. Cokey sat down across from them.

"Well, I didn't tell you everything," Katherine admitted.

Jake asked, "What happened?"

"There was someone in the house. They had a hoodie on. I couldn't see who it was. I chased them out the front door."

"Man or woman?" Cokey asked.

"I couldn't tell. The person was stocky, kind of like that Russian Misha guy. I think he's the one who stole Iris."

Cokey scratched his head, "Why the hell would he want your cat?"

Jake shook his head. "Nope, Katz, Misha doesn't have Iris."

"What do you mean?" Katherine asked in doubt.

"When I pulled the Jeep on the shoulder and tried to find a way out of the traffic jam, Officer Glover stopped me. He said the motorhome owner was dead. I could see the paramedics loading a body bag into the ambulance. Katz, Misha is dead."

Katherine and Colleen gasped. "Oh, no way," Katherine said. "Why?"

"Officer Glover said he'd been strangled."

"Oh, the saints preserve us," Colleen said, running out of the room.

Katherine's voice broke. "But he had to have taken Iris, because Scout did her . . . ," Katherine choked, then stopped. Cokey and Jake didn't know about Scout's special skill. "I've got to get a hold of the chief and have him look for Iris in the motorhome. She has to be there."

Colleen came back into the room, "Katz, there's something I need to tell you. During the party, before the scavenger hunt began, I went upstairs to my room. On my way back to the party, I heard a male voice say, "Give it to me. It's mine." Then I heard Misha say, "Make a bizz-ness." By the time I got downstairs, there was no one in sight."

Cokey asked Colleen, "You didn't recognize the voice?"

"No, why should I?" Colleen said throwing up her hands. "I just thought it was one of the people involved with the catering, because the party guests had headed to the basement."

Jake said to Katherine, "Are you going to be okay for a little while? Cokey and I are driving over to the mansion to check things out."

Cokey agreed, "Yeah, the chief ain't gonna be available anytime soon. He's got his hands full."

Katherine disagreed. "I don't think the two of you should do that. I think we should leave Colleen and the cats here and go back to the mansion to wait for the police."

"Ain't happening," Cokey said, getting up. He briskly left the room.

Realizing she wasn't going to win the argument, Katherine reached into her pocket and yanked out her house keys. Handing them to Jake, she said, "Please promise you'll wait for the police?"

Jake leaned down and kissed Katherine on the nose. "Lock up. I'll text when I'm coming back. Oh, and by the way, I plan on staying the night. So, could you make up that sofa in the front room?"

"Sure," Katherine said.

After Cokey and Jake left, Katherine locked both of the front door locks. When she returned to the kitchen, Colleen was rooting around in the refrigerator.

Katherine read her mind and said, "There's some Guinness in the very back. Pour me a glass, too."

Colleen took out two bottles and flipped their caps. "How about drinking straight from the bottle? I'm in that kind of a mood," she laughed, then asked, "Where am I sleeping?"

Katherine answered, "The official guest room is the first bedroom on the right. It's got hardly any furniture in it but a bed and dresser. The sheets are in the bottom drawer. Follow me. I'll help you make up your bed before I make up the sofa."

As they walked down the short hallway to the bedroom, they heard glass breaking in the front dining room. The cats began wailing in Katherine's bedroom. "Shhh," Katherine said to Colleen. She grabbed her arm and led her back to the kitchen.

Katherine reached behind the small of her back and extracted her Glock. She motioned for Colleen to get behind her. She immediately turned off the kitchen counter light. They could hear someone breaking more glass to crawl inside the window.

226

"I know you're in here, you little bitch," the male voice said. "Where the hell are you?" He stumbled over one of the dining room chairs.

Katherine brought her finger to her lips to silently "shhh" Colleen. She motioned Colleen to crawl underneath the built-in table. While Colleen scurried under the table, Katherine quietly moved to the open kitchen door and stood beside it.

The intruder crept through the guest bedroom doorway and switched off the overhead light. He was dressed entirely in black, with a shaved head and gold earring. The hood of his jacket was down around his collar. Then he slowly moved to the second bedroom. There he made the mistake of opening the door to the cats.

A frenzied pair of seal-point Siamese catapulted out of the room. Abra went for the man's belt, and Scout sprang for his head. Horrible feline screeches began while the man tried to remove the attacking cats. Distracted, he dropped a tire iron on the floor and didn't see Katherine inching closer from behind. Katherine remembered the gun instructor's sage advice, "Never put your finger on the trigger unless you mean to use it." She said in a firm tone, "I've got a Glock aimed at the back of your head. Slowly drop to your knees and put your hands behind your head, or I'll shoot *you* in a *New York minute*."

The student Glen Frye knelt on the hallway floor and did what Katherine told him to do. Katherine kicked the tire iron and it went skidding down the hallway, out of arm's reach. Colleen ran from the kitchen, switched on the hall light, and grabbed her cell. She punched in 9-1-1. "Get the police over here immediately. A man broke into the house and my friend has a gun on him! Katz Kendall. I mean Katherine Kendall. We're at the bungalow! Wait I'll find out," Colleen said to Katherine. "What's the address here?"

"205 Alexander Street," Katherine answered.

Colleen repeated the address into the phone. "Okay, I'll leave the cell on until the police get here. Thanks." She set the phone down on a side table, per the 9-1-1 operator's instructions.

Katherine said to Colleen, "I saw Scout and Abra run back into their room. If Lilac and Abby are in there, can you shut the door?"

Colleen took a wide berth of Glen and observed the four cats inside. She quickly shut the door.

Glen struggled to get up but Katherine kicked him in the lower back. "Hey, I'm a crack shot! Now stay the hell down!"

Colleen and Katherine could hear police sirens in the distance. Colleen rushed over to stand by the front door.

Hearing the sirens, Katherine thought, *I do hope they're coming over here first, and not to the mansion.*

Glen said slyly to Katherine, "You've got something that belongs to me. If you give it to me and let me go, I'll tell you where your cat is."

"I don't have anything of yours," she said doubtfully.

"Yes, you do," Glen said in a low voice. "I saw you pick it up on the roof and put it in your pocket."

Katherine wondered where Glen had to be in order to have observed her, then remembered how she picked up an envelope on the roof outside her bedroom window. Fishing in her pocket with her free hand, she tugged it out. As she tore open the envelope with her teeth, a gold charm bracelet fell out in her hand. 'I Luv Mommy' was engraved on the charm. Katherine said with growing disgust, "You stole this from Stacy when you assaulted her. What kind of sicko are you?"

"I didn't steal it. She got the car door open and I lunged to stop her. The bracelet came off in my hand. Look," he pleaded, "Just hand it over and I'll tell you about your cat. Don't you want to know?"

Suddenly Katherine got a sick feeling deep in her stomach. *What if he killed her*, she thought, then asked skeptically, "What does *he* look like? Is *he* fat or skinny? When *he* sits up is *he* tall or short?"

"He's tall and skinny," he said.

"Liar!" Katherine exploded. She knew Glen was referring to the day Scout and Abra strolled into the classroom. They were both tall. "You were standing outside my room and heard me say my cat was missing."

"Wait a minute," Glen pleaded. "I didn't see the cat, but I heard it. That damn Russian had it in his Four Winds, locked up in the back. It was howling like a banshee."

"What were you doing in Misha's motorhome? Did you kill him?" Katherine accused. She wondered if there was any truth to Glen's story about the cat, then said, "Just shut up until the police get here." She dropped the bracelet back into the envelope.

Colleen opened the front door and directed the Erie police to the back hall. Chief London and an officer Katherine didn't recognize dashed in. Cokey and Jake sprinted in after them.

The chief said to Katherine, "Ms. Kendall, I'm here now. You can put the gun down."

For a moment, Katherine was so caught up in an adrenaline rush, she continued pointing the gun at Glen.

"Katz, put the gun down," Jake said emphatically. Katherine snapped out of it, held the gun out at arm's length, muzzle pointed up, and set it slowly on the side table.

Chief London stooped down and handcuffed Glen. "Stand up," he barked. Glen tried, but wasn't able, so the chief and the other officer helped him to his feet. The chief frisked him, yanking out his wallet and cell phone. He also found a high school ring with the initials J. G. on it. He tugged a blue latex glove on and removed an evidence bag from his pocket. He dropped the items inside and handed the bag to the officer.

"Well lookie here," the chief said gruffly. "Mr. Frye. You're just the man I've been lookin' for."

Glen threw the chief a venomous look and threatened, "You've got nothin' on me."

"Is that a fact? Enjoy taking souvenirs from your victims? This ring belongs to Jane Gilroy. Remember her? The last woman you murdered?"

Katherine handed the chief the scavenger hunt envelope. "Chief, inside is the bracelet belonging to Stacy Grimes. Glen just said it fell off when Stacy jumped out of his car. One of my party entertainers was a close-up magician who lifted things from my guests' pockets —"

The chief interrupted impatiently, "Okay, I know this is leading somewhere."

"The bracelet was in Glen's pocket; Misha the magician pickpocketed it. I suspect that when Glen tried to get it back, Misha wanted money for it. Glen wasn't able to buy it, so he came back later to the mansion to look for it."

"You lying bitch," Glen muttered.

"You can't talk to her like that," Jake said, throwing a punch at Glen, but Cokey blocked it.

Katherine explained. "Chief, the last time I saw Stacy Grimes, she said the father of her child had given the bracelet to her."

"Is this true, Mr. Frye?" the chief asked, irritably. "Are you the daddy?"

"I ain't that kid's father."

"This is the way I see it, Mr. Frye," the chief began. "You somehow managed to get the magician to drive you to the Sanders trailer court. Then you strangled him. You called my niece Tiffany to come and pick you up, but she declined."

"That's a freakin' lie!"

"I've got a text message on my phone that says otherwise. Why did you call Tiffany? Was she going to be your next victim?"

"You're crazy," Glen said.

"It's only a matter of time till I find out who picked you up and drove you back to the pink mansion," the chief said. "Someone else working with you?"

"I hitched a ride. I don't know who the hell it was, some trucker. Hey, I'm getting a lawyer," Glen swore. "I'm gonna sue you, the town, and that witch with the cats. I need to see a doc for my wounds. Can't you see I'm bleeding? Better hope they don't have rabies, Katz!" he threatened. "Because if they do, they'll get the needle."

Katherine was speechless. *The man is pure evil*, she thought.

"Getting a lawyer is the smartest thing you've said," the chief advised, then read Glen the Miranda warning.

After the chief finished, Glen said sullenly, "You're wasting your time. I'm innocent."

"Let's see," the chief said, tugging at his beard. "Possession of a crime victim's personal belonging is good evidence. But you ain't heard nothin' yet. Stacy Grimes is alive. She's out of her coma. And she's talking. You don't have a leg to stand on."

Another cruiser parked in front of the bungalow. Officer Glover got out of the car and hurried into the house. The chief said, "Dan, help Officer Troy take Mr. Frye down to the station so we can question him. Make sure he gets medical help for his cat scratches." The two escorted the former computer class student to the Erie police station.

The chief lingered behind. He said, "I've got a strong suspicion, Ms. Kendall, you've just single-handedly caught the Festival Murderer. Or should I include the cats, too? They seem to have done a number on Mr. Frye. Would you like to come and work for us?"

Katherine shook her head, "No, but thanks for offering."

The chief patted her on the back, "Good work!" he praised. "I want to talk to you more about this, but I've got other fires to put out. Gotta get a hold of the task force and do a million other things. How about I get your statement in the morning?" he asked, walking to the front door.

"Chief, what about the tire iron Glen broke in with. I kicked it to the back of the hall."

The chief walked back and pulled out a larger evidence bag. He carefully picked up the tire iron and slipped the bag over it. He scratched his head.

"Gut-feeling is Glen probably used this to overpower those poor women before he strangled them. I'll make sure Detective Martin knows about this."

Katherine nodded, but then said hurriedly, "Before you leave, can you give me information about the Four Winds motorhome you found, belonging to the Russian, Misha? Did anyone report seeing or finding a Siamese cat? Several hours ago she was stolen from my house. Glen said my cat was locked up in a back room in Misha's motorhome."

"Well, Ms. Kendall, that intel certainly places Glen in the motorhome with the victim."

Katherine said excitedly, "I need to go and see if my cat's there."

"Hold on there, hot shot," the chief insisted. He removed his smartphone from his belt clip and called someone. He spoke for a moment and then reattached the phone to his belt. "I'm sorry to be the bearer of bad news, but *there wasn't* a cat in the motorhome. Gotta head out," he said, leaving.

"If Glen was lying about my cat, I have reason to believe Barbie Sanders stole her."

"Barbie Sanders, you said? She's in a holding cell right now. She's the town's egger. We found her with her brother egging the mayor's house. Caught in the act! Her car was full of eggs from out-of-town. I'll ask her about your cat, but I'm bankin' she didn't do it."

"Appreciate it," Katherine said.

"Good evening," the chief said to Colleen, as he walked out the door.

Jake gathered Katherine in his arms and said, "I was so worried something awful had happened to you. How did that nutcase know you were at the bungalow?"

Colleen offered, "He was standing outside the bedroom door when Katz said we were coming over here. But all Katz said was 'bungalow.' How did he know the address?"

"Small town, Colleen," Jake answered. "People know everything about everybody."

"I guess my secret 'getaway house from the mansion' isn't so secret, after all," Katherine said with resignation. She buried her face in Jake's chest. "Well, I hope I never have to apprehend a crim again, but at least I didn't have to fire a shot."

Colleen collapsed in a nearby Morris chair. She said in an exaggerated Irish accent, "I thought we'd all be killed."

Jake kissed Katherine on the forehead, "Your gun instructor would be proud! I've got to leave for a short while. I got to find Cokey and patch up that broken window. We can't stay here tonight with it open."

Colleen added, "Oh, Cokey's gone. He left right after the officers hauled Mr. Clean away." She caught herself and said, "Shut the door, Katz! Do you remember the web search . . . ?"

Katherine shot her a look and mouthed the word *No*. Jake had turned and didn't see the gesture.

"Oh, never mind. I'm just running at the mouth," Colleen said, recovering.

Jake looked momentarily confused. "I'll be back in a minute. I need to see if Cokey needs any help hauling the plywood over here." He left, still with an inquisitive look of "what the hell did that mean?" on his face.

"Katz, why did you shush me when I mentioned Mr. Clean and the Internet search?"

"I'd kind of like to keep this between you and me. I haven't told Jake about the cats' special sleuthing abilities, however they work. We know they're special, but Jake doesn't. For the time being,

I want him to think they're ordinary housecats. Let's just take it one day at a time."

Colleen agreed. "Of course, Katz. My lips are sealed. Do you really think I should leave Monday? I'm worried about you."

"Don't worry. I'm good. I've got a Glock," Katherine said lightly, trying to put her friend at ease.

"Seriously, Katz, please come back to Manhattan," Colleen implored. "Your living in this place scares me to death. I think you're safer in Manhattan. You can have your old apartment back. Jacky and I would gladly move back in with Mum."

"How do you know that bad luck wouldn't follow me back to NYC? Besides, I have people in Erie I care about. Jake, Cokey, Margie and their kids. My new friends."

Colleen replied with a wink. "Mostly Jake. What was with the diamond ring in his pocket? Is he going to pop a question?"

Katherine shook her head. "I don't have a clue. Colleen, I've only got four more months, and I'll inherit my great aunt's fortune. I'll decide then whether I want to stay here or move somewhere else."

"Ma-waugh," Scout agreed from behind the door of Katherine's bedroom.

Colleen laughed nervously.

Katherine said sadly, worrying about Iris, "When Jake comes back, I'm going to ask him to drive me to the Sanders trailer court. I want to look for her."

"I'm so sorry about Iris," Colleen comforted.

"I won't have a moment's peace until I find her," Katherine assured.

"I know," Colleen said, beginning to choke up.

"I won't either."

Chapter Eight

It was a bitterly cold day. The wind whipped up and down Lincoln Street, blowing leaves out of the piles that residents had made on either side of the street for the town's vacuum leaf removal truck. The leaves scattered down the hill with each gust. The wind chill made the outside thirty-eight degrees feel even colder. Katherine bundled up in layers to finish the leaf raking chore. Cokey said he would hire someone to do the strenuous task, but she declined. She told him it would do her good. "Great exercise," she explained. Cokey had looked at her like she'd lost her mind, but didn't persist. He was aware that Katherine was mourning the loss of Iris, who had been missing for two weeks.

Katherine hadn't given up hope. She'd driven to the Erie animal shelter twice a day and checked to see if Iris had been turned in. She knew she was annoying the limited staff, who assured her they'd call if Iris showed up, but it was too painful to wait for a call that never came. The shelter lacked the funds to be a no-kill facility, so Katherine vowed she'd change that once she got her inheritance. Scout, Abra, Lilac and Abby missed their friend. They sensed that all was not right with their human, and clung to her even more.

The evening when Iris first went missing, Katherine and Jake drove to the location of the Misha's motorhome, but the state police wouldn't let them search inside. When they arrived, the motorhome was being jacked up by a special tow truck, and was impounded for further evidence gathering. The officers were sympathetic, but swore there wasn't a cat inside. They said they'd checked every nook and cranny. No cat. No Iris.

The next day, Katherine created and printed flyers with Iris's picture on it to post all over town. Jake's family rallied behind Katherine in searching for the Siamese. Cokey, Margie and the kids went door-to-door asking residents if they'd seen the missing feline. Even Jake's unfriendly mother warmed up to Katz and, with Jake's dad, pounded the streets of Erie, alerting the residents about the missing cat. Colleen and Daryl drove out to the Sanders trailer court and tacked up a poster there. At first, some of the residents were suspicious, but once they knew the flyer was about a missing pet, they allowed them to post one on a telephone pole outside the entrance.

Katherine offered a reward. The flyer stated: With the safe return of my seal-point Siamese, you shall have one thousand dollars in cash. The reward brought a barrage of phone calls. Katherine followed up with each one. The usual scenario was that someone would call stating they'd seen Iris. Katherine would jump in her car, drive to the caller's place, and then be disappointed when the cat turned out to be a tabby cat or some breed other than a

Siamese. When Jake was able, he'd go along on these trips and comfort her when she got home. But today, Jake was teaching. It was Friday, and she wouldn't see him until later in the evening.

Colleen had flown back to Manhattan, but called or texted every day, asking about Iris and giving Katz moral support. The estate's lawyer, Mark Dunn, suggested a television spot in the city during the evening news, but Katherine declined. She reasoned that the city was so far away, and that if Iris had escaped the motorhome, she'd still be in the Erie area. Detective Martin, who also loved cats, took a flyer and posted it at the state police headquarters. Many officers promised to be alert to finding the missing pet.

Katherine had her back to the street when the pickup truck pulled up. Turning to see who it was, and expecting to see either Margie or Cokey in their Dodge Ram, she was surprised to see Sam Sanders, Erie's best approximation of a "crime boss" behind the wheel, with his daughter, Barbie, riding shotgun. Katherine couldn't imagine what they could possibly want, but stood staring at them until Sam got out and came over.

"Ms. Kendall, I think we got off on the wrong foot," he said kindly. He wore a black jacket, white dress shirt, and dark blue jeans. His beard was closely cropped. He looked very handsome, but his ice-blue eyes seemed to tell an ominous tale. "I've thought back on that day I offered you a bribe, and I've kicked myself a million times. You must think I'm a horrid man."

Katherine turned and leaned the rake up against the magnolia tree. "What can I do for you?" she asked.

"My daughter and I just got back in town. I was in Chicago for a couple of weeks and Barbie and her brother Bobby were up at Lake Monty staying in the family cabin. I have a true story to tell and it's a good one. I don't want you to jump to any conclusions until you've heard me out."

"Okay," Katherine said, wondering what a crime boss would tell her. She gazed at the truck and at Barbie, who was staring straight ahead like she was in some kind of trance. She wondered why she didn't get out and join the conversation.

Sam Sanders ran his hand through his hair. "I've got connections in town. I know you told the police that my daughter broke in your house and stole your cat."

Katherine began in a solemn voice. "I was upset about a number of things and made accusations I shouldn't have made." She thought, *I was desperate to find Iris — and holding a gun on the serial killer until the chief got there.*

"Do you know how I know it wasn't my daughter who took your cat?" He waited for Katherine to answer, but when she didn't, he said,

"Much to my embarrassment, Barbie was out with her numbskull brother, egging the damn Mayor's house. Now how stupid is that?"

Katherine shrugged, but didn't offer what she was really thinking, which was Barbie didn't seem to have too much in the brain department. "I was wrong. It is *I* who owe you an apology, to you, your family, and to Barbie." Katherine started to walk to the truck, but Sam gently placed his hand on her right elbow.

"Let me finish and then you can talk to Barbie. Okay?"

"Yes, please go on," she said with a slight edge in her voice.

"When that idiot Glen Frye dumped the motorhome in our trailer court, we got to it before the law did. The guy I hire to take care of the place lives in the first trailer. He wondered why the hell a

Four Winds motorhome with New York license plates would be blocking most of the front entrance, so he investigated. He said when he went inside, a cat flew out and nearly knocked him down."

"Did he chase after her?" Katherine asked, with renewed hope of finding Iris. "Does he have her?"

Sam shook his head and smiled. "I couldn't see Homer chasing anything but the dinner roll basket down at the diner. Actually, he was more concerned about the dead man in the RV than chasing after a cat." He paused, then continued, "Now here's where my story gets interesting. After my eldest son bailed out Barbie and Bobby from jail, I called my daughter. I told her it would be best if she and her brother got out of town for a while and stayed at the cabin. But Barbie didn't mention to me that there was a third party going to the lake."

"What do you mean?" Katherine asked, anxious for Sam Sanders to get to the point.

"My daughter loves animals. She's always taking in a stray cat or dog, fixing them up, and then adopting them out. The night Barbie got home and opened her front door, a freaked-out cat ran into her trailer. As soon as she could calm it down, she put it in a cage and headed up north to the lake. She told me it was love at first sight."

"Was the cat a Siamese?" Katherine asked hurriedly.

Sam put up his hand. "I'm not finished yet," he said firmly. "Like I said, my daughter took the cat with her. We didn't know the cat was *your* cat until Barbie got home today. She saw the flyer outside the trailer court, and called me —"

Katherine interrupted. "Where's the cat now? I want to see if it's my cat."

Sam motioned for Barbie to get out of the truck. Barbie slowly opened the door and climbed out. In her arms, she was holding something wrapped in a yellow baby blanket. Tears were flowing from Barbie's eyes. She was so choked up, she couldn't speak. Iris peeked out and made a joyous yowl. Barbie handed the missing Siamese to Katherine, then ran back to the truck, sobbing.

"So, are we good here?" Sam asked, touching Katherine on the shoulder.

"Yes," Katherine cried. "How can I ever repay you? The reward . . . ," she stammered. "It's yours."

"We'll take care of that later. But for now, I do ask one thing," Sam said softly. "Teach Barbie about that computer stuff and we'll be *clear*."

"Yes, of course. We're clear. I'll give her private lessons."

"Good," Sam said, starting to walk away. "You take care now," he said, getting into his truck and driving away. Barbie had her head down, still crying.

Katherine cradled Iris and kissed her several times on the head. Scout and Abra were moving back and forth on the parlor windowsill, wanting to get out. When Katherine walked in the door, Lilac and Abby began me-yowling and chirping with excitement that Iris had been found. Scout and Abra joined them. She could hardly walk with the cats wrapped around her feet, darting in and out between her legs.

"Yowl," Iris cried to the other cats' caterwauling. She squirmed to get down, but Katherine held her tight.

"Not yet, Miss Siam. I've got to check you out to make sure you're okay." Katherine set Iris down on the marble-top curio cabinet and began examining her. Iris seemed to be all right. She smelled like perfume, but that was an easy fix. She seemed to be a little bit heavier. Katherine guessed Barbie had been over-feeding her. She extracted her smartphone and snapped a picture of Iris, then sent it to Jake and Colleen. Jake immediately replied with a selfie of himself smiling; Colleen texted back: "Happy dancing!" Katherine then called Dr. Sonny. Valerie, the receptionist, put the call straight through.

"Dr. Sonny, I've got Iris. Barbie Sanders had her and was taking care of her."

"Oh, really," Dr. Sonny said, mildly amused.

"She seems okay, but I really want to bring her in for you to take a look at her."

"If she looks okay, I'd suggest you do that tomorrow. Let her get settled in. I'm sure this was a great shock to her. Maybe you should keep her away from the cats for a while."

"Okay, sure thing. Tomorrow," Katherine said, ending the call. Surprisingly, the once-noisy cats had become quiet. With Scout in the lead, they ran upstairs to their room in the back of the hall.

Katherine picked up Iris and cradled her in her arms. She walked back to the office and closed the door. "Miss Siam, have I ever told you the story about how you became royalty?"

"Yowl," Iris cried softly, blinking her deep blue eyes.

Katherine sat down on the floor and put Iris on her lap. She began talking to the Siamese as she had when Iris was a kitten. Iris gazed up at her adoringly. "Once upon a time, in Siam, there was a little cat. Her name was Iris. She had a brown mask with big, dark blue eyes. She was a member of the royal guard that stood as sentries on the tall city walls. The royal princess of Siam didn't like her because she said Iris had stolen her favorite ring. But Iris hadn't. It was Chai-Lai, the wicked Siamese, who did it."

Iris reached up with her paw and touched Katherine on the face.

"One night there was a fire and Iris saved the princess," Katherine continued the story.

Iris was falling asleep; her eyelids were very heavy.

"After Iris saved the princess, there was a ceremony and Iris was crowned. Do you know what her new title was?"

Iris looked up sleepily.

"Miss Siam – Royal Guard to the Princess."

Iris cuddled closer and fell fast asleep.

"I'm so glad you're home, my darling. I love you so very much," Katherine said, fighting back tears. "But you're safe now – in my arms – so just sleep. I'll hold you forever."

The End

Dear Reader . . .

Thank you so much for reading my book. I hope you enjoyed reading it as much as I did writing it. If you liked, *The Cats that Told a Fortune*, I would be so thankful if you'd help others enjoy this book, too, by recommending it to your friends, family and book clubs, and/or by writing a positive review on Amazon and/or Goodreads.

I love it when my readers write to me. If you'd like to email me about what you'd like to see in the next book, or just talk about your favorite scenes and characters, email me at:
karenannegolden@gmail.com

Amazon author page:
http://www.amazon.com/Karen-Anne-Golden/e/B00H3KTH8Q/ref=ntt_athr_dp_pel_1

My Facebook author page is:
https://www.facebook.com/karenannegolden

If you're not on my mailing list, please send me an email and I'll let you know when the next book is available.

Thanks again!

Karen Anne Golden

The Cats that Surfed the Web

Book One in *The Cats that . . .* Cozy Mystery series

If you haven't read the first book, *The Cats that Surfed the Web*, you can download the Kindle version on Amazon at: http://amzn.com/B00H2862YG Paperback available.

Forty four million dollars. A Victorian mansion. And a young career woman with cats. The prospect sounded like a dream come true; what could possibly go wrong?

How could a friendly town's welcome turn into a case of poisoning, murder, and deceit? When Katherine "Katz" Kendall, a computer professional in New York City, discovers she's the sole heir of a huge inheritance, she can't believe her good fortune. She's okay with the clauses of the will: Move to the small town of Erie, Indiana, check. Live in her great aunt's pink Victorian mansion and take care of an Abyssinian cat, double-check.

With her three Siamese cats and best friend, Colleen, riding shotgun, Katz leaves Manhattan to find a former housekeeper dead in the basement. Ghostly intrusions convince Colleen, a card-carrying "ghost hunter," that the mansion is haunted. Several townspeople are furious because Katherine's benefactor promised them the fortune, then changed her will at the last minute. But who would be greedy enough to get rid of the rightful heir to take the money and run? Four adventurous felines help Katz solve the crimes by serendipitously "searching" the Internet for clues.

The Cats that Chased the Storm

Book Two in *The Cats that . . .* Cozy Mystery series

The second book, *The Cats that Chased the Storm*, is also available on Kindle and in paperback. Amazon: http://amzn.com/B00IPOPJOU

It's early May in Erie, Indiana, and the weather has turned most foul. We find Katherine "Katz" Kendall, heiress to the Colfax fortune, living in a pink mansion, caring for her three Siamese and Abby the Abyssinian. Severe thunderstorms frighten the cats, but Scout is better than any weather app. A different storm is brewing, however, with a discovery that connects great-uncle William Colfax to the notorious gangster John Dillinger. Why is the Erie Historical Society so eager to get William's personal papers? Is the new man in Katherine's life a fortune hunter? Will Abra mysteriously reappear, and is Abby a magnet for danger?

A fast-paced whodunit, the second book in *The Cats that . . .* series involves four extraordinary felines that help Katz unravel the mysteries in her life.

Made in United States
North Haven, CT
17 February 2023

32699349R10153